The Adventurer's Bond

Book 5 of Adventures on Brad

by

Tao Wong

Copyright

This is a work of fiction. Names, characters, businesses, places, events and incidents are either the products of the author's imagination or used in a fictitious manner. Any resemblance to actual persons, living or dead, or actual events is purely coincidental.

This book is licensed for your personal enjoyment only. This book may not be re-sold or given away to other people. If you would like to share this book with another person, please purchase an additional copy for each recipient. If you're reading this book and did not purchase it, or it was not purchased for your use only, then please return to your favorite book retailer and purchase your own copy. Thank you for respecting the hard work of this author.

Books in the Adventures on Brad series

A Healer's Gift
An Adventurer's Heart
A Dungeon's Soul
The Arena's Call
The Adventurer's Bond
The Forest's Silence

Contents

Chapter 1

The party of five Adventurers traversed the first level of Porthos - one of Silverstone's three dungeons - carefully, heads swivelling in slow order as they checked their surroundings. The six-foot-wide walkway of stone they walked upon joined one magically-levitated platform to another, crossing empty space at a stomach-churning height. Below, wisps of mist hid and revealed additional platforms and walkways beneath them. On occasion, the screech of an imp or the low chittering sounds of their conversation floated upward to the party.

A stout figure in simple brown and green leather moved at the head of the group, bow held in one hand and a trio of arrows in the other. Occasionally, the figure would stop and crouch low as it stared at the ground before rising and moving forward again with a small wave of their hand. Brown hair, shorn short and rough along the skull, framed a pair of liquid brown eyes, a slightly curved nose and thin lips. A small scar bisected one eyebrow, giving the teenage Ranger a more sinister air.

"We will not clear this floor at this rate," rumbled Omrak, the large blond barbarian from the North, as he walked behind the Ranger, his massive two-handed sword held in hand and resting on his shoulder. Sheathed alongside his enchanted, soft leather tunic was a trio of throwing axes, held in place by a simple leather baldric. Along one tree-trunk sized leg a short sword hung, appearing deceptively small, like a large knife, strapped to his thigh.

The Ranger stiffened slightly before continuing to move at her original slow pace. Daniel rubbed his nose with his shield hand, briefly blocking his view. In his other hand, the rockbow rested lightly, waiting for Daniel to load and fire the specialized weapon as he trudged just behind Omrak. He looked over at the youngster and decided – once again – against requesting the barbarian to speak softer.

"We're here to learn to work together, Omrak, not clear the floor," Daniel consoled the Northerner softly. "I'd rather we learn to do so here than in Artos. At least here we know the dangers."

"A good decision," the Mage who walked directly beside Daniel agreed. He turned sideways, smiling ingratiatingly at Daniel while he waved a ringed hand at their surroundings. Daniel noted once again the surprisingly calloused and scarred pair of hands, a contrast to the refined appearance other Mages often showcased. Dark, glistening hair and a beard adorned the Mage's head, hair once again slicked back by the waving hand after he finished gesturing. "Though our companion's speed is low."

"Trap-finding," Asin, the only Catkin member of the five, said. Her tail waved behind her lazily as she watched the back of the group from her position ten steps behind, her keen senses having picked up the conversation between the trio. Unlike the heavily armed and armored pair, the Catkin had on a light leather brigandine that covered her torso, a short cloak and crisscrossing baldrics of throwing knives across her body. More throwing knives sat on her thighs and upper arms, and a pair of larger knives sat on her hips for close-combat.

"But there is only one type of trap on this floor," said Omrak. "We should be seeking battle!"

"If you don't quieten down, I'm sure we'll find some," the Mage replied with a grimace and turned back to his side of the walkway to scan for trouble.

"I am quiet, Rob," Omrak hissed insistently, even going so far as to turn around to glare at the Mage. Instead, he met Daniel's placid brown eyes.

"Eyes forward, Omrak. You know better," Daniel said. The Northerner flushed but nodded, swinging back around and hurrying to get back into line, eyeing both the empty skies and the misty clouds below. Eventually, the quintet made their way to a larger, more stable platform where Daniel held a hand up, signalling a stop.

"Alright. I think that's enough for now. Thank you, Tula," Daniel said. The Ranger bobbed her head slightly, accepting Daniel's words and making him smile slightly. Tula amused him as the young lady was a happy, outspoken woman outside the dungeon. But inside, she became as quiet and taciturn as Asin. "It looks like your trap detecting abilities are slower than Asin's. Maybe it's because they're more suited for the outdoors. Either way, I'd like to adjust our positioning."

"Finally," Omrak grumbled.

Ignoring the blond, Daniel continued to speak. "Asin, you take the front. Omrak will be behind her, ten feet back. Tula, you and Rob will be in the middle to provide ranged support. I'll take the back."

When he received confirmation from the group about their new formation, Daniel smiled. So far, at least, there had not been any major conflicts of personalities. Luckily, they were all Advanced adventurers and as such, each had some modicum of experience in Dungeons. The idiots, the foolhardy hotheads and those who could not work in teams did not often progress pass Beginner Dungeons.

"Let's rest here for ten minutes, and then we'll try to push for the Floor Champion."

Omrak grinned widely at these words while the others just nodded in affirmation. As the group spread out to watch one corner of the platform each, they reached for their trail rations, pulling from their inventory water and a simple mixtures of nuts, fruits and dried meat. Daniel noted how Tula, while not having the actual Adventurer Class, had a Skill of her own which allowed her to conveniently store her belongings in the small satchel by her side.

"Enchanted holding?" Asin asked, her head cocked curiously to the side when she saw Rob pull his rations from a pendant on his chest.

"Yes," Rob said, touching the pendant. "A gift from my Master." There was a hint of warning in his voice, a sign that avarice towards this item would bring significant consequences from an irate Master Mage.

"Expensive?" Asin said.

"Very much so. Enchanted work like this is in extreme demand because it requires a significant understanding of spatial magic," Rob said. "It is a specialized field and is expensive to develop. More so than other forms of enchanting."

Daniel nodded slowly. He absently wondered if spatial magic was a specialization of a Class which would be made available at Level 20 or if it was just an area of focus. Of course, he did not ask, as Classes could be a touchy subject. The Focused, in particular, were touchy about levels. The Focused were people like Tula who had received and stuck to a single Class since their age of majority, a choice made when their initial 'Minor' Class had been given up. This allowed the Focused to gain significant levels since they were not 'splitting' their experience gain across multiple Classes. It did, however, reduce the variety of Skills they had access to and made it simpler to grasp their strength if their Levels were known. As such, discussing Classes and Skills in detail were anathema to the Focused.

In truth, Daniel considered the Focused the lucky ones – able to choose a profession when they reached their age of majority rather than have one forced upon them like most Farmers, Miners and those of the lower classes. Certainly, there were Focused Miners, but they were more often a case of circumstance than choice. They certainly did not go about flaunting their status. Not that Tula or Rob had. Yet.

Conversation petered out soon after, the quartet chewing and drinking quickly while allowing their bodies to rest. It was Tula who first noticed the incoming horde - a swarm of three-foot-tall, red-skinned creatures with black claws and web-like wings. Tula let out a low cry of warning as she swiftly stood, her bow in hand and an arrow snatched from the ground where it had been stuck point first.

"Two dozen," Tula reported as she squinted. She frowned slightly, spotting a much larger Imp lagging behind the swarm of red-skinned, black-clawed flying monsters. Swiftly, she drew the string to her cheek and fired, grasping a second arrow immediately even as the Ranger activated her first Skill, **Arrow Storm**.

This was the first time Daniel had a chance to observe the Ranger's Skill. **Arrow Storm** created multiple temporary copies from a single arrow which flew in a wide or tight arrangement around the original as desired by its user. With time and experience, Tula would be able to guide those impermanent arrows to their target better, but for now, they flew unguided in a wide formation towards the Imps. Even so, the swarm of imps was forced to take evasive action, flapping their tiny wings as they dodged the incoming projectiles, leaving only a pair injured, one fatally. Still, the attack gave the other Adventurers the break they required.

Rockbow braced against his shoulder, Daniel exhaled before pulling the trigger. The rockbow was a modified crossbow that threw explosive rocks into the air, sending tiny shards flying towards the Imps. The weapon was nothing more than an annoyance to larger creatures but to the smaller Imps with their fragile wings, it could be deadly as Daniel showcased. Already turning aside from the initial attack by Tula, a trio of Imps were caught and bunched tightly together when the Adventurer fired. The crack of the stone flying through the air and the shriek of the Imps accompanied each other as the rocks shred the thin membranes of the creatures' wings. In a second, the trio of monsters were sent spiraling into the abyss below.

With the two dedicated ranged weapons unleashed, the Imps flapped their wings quicker as they wheeled around, lining up to tear into the party. It was then that they met the next layer of the Adventurers' defenses. Firstly, Asin's throwing knives flashed in the pale blue Mana light of the Dungeon, catching the monsters in their chests as they unerringly struck their target. Each knife carried with it a small charge from the Catkin's lightning-enchanted bracers, shocking the monsters, long enough for Omrak to wield his oversized sword to slice apart the distracted monsters as they were gliding in.

Once the remaining Imps made it past Omrak, Daniel was ready with his shield to defend himself and Rob. Rather than drop his rockbow, the Adventurer focused on defense at the moment, hoping to get a second effective shot with the weapon when the Imps passed by.

In addition, star-shaped and pointed enchanted spikes activated around Rob, flying forwards and homing in on the nearest Imps. Even a last-minute jerk from the monsters was too slow, allowing each of the pair of enchanted defenses to tear into and exit the monster's chests. Together, the pair of darts wove their way through the air around the mage. This last defense deterred all but the bravest of monsters, forcing them off. And those which refused to back off were Shield Bashed aside by Daniel.

Monsters which fell to the ground were quickly dispatched by the Adventurers, facing death by knife, sword or boot. Working together, the quintet made short work of the larger than normal swarm of Imps. As the Imps dissolved into blue motes, leaving behind tiny Mana stones, Daniel found himself exhaling with relief. At least no one stabbed anyone else in the back. Literally or figuratively.

"Mine!" Asin growled at Rob who was in the process of storing a few looted Mana stones in a pouch by his side.

"This is a party pouch," Rob said, his back straightening at the Catkin's tone. "I have separated my personal funds from it."

"Actually, we generally let Asin store and track the stones," Daniel said hesitantly.

"That makes no logical sense. If the Catkin were to fall into a trap or her corpse be otherwise irretrievable, we would lose all our earnings," Rob protested. "It is illogical to not split our collection."

"Well, it's what we've done before," Daniel muttered. He grimaced slightly, realising he didn't know how to explain the reason for the rule to Rob. At least without potentially insulting his long-time Catkin friend. After all, he had allowed Asin to collect the stones because she liked doing so. And Omrak had never protested, being the easy-going individual that he was. After that, it just had become habit.

"Traditions are but shackles of the past," Rob said. "I am not convinced on the need for our scout – the most vulnerable member of our party

— to be entrusted with the full extent of our earnings."

"Look, let's go with our party rules for now and discuss changes once we are out of the dungeon," Daniel said.

"Very well. My protest is, however, lodged," Rob said before he fished the stones out from his pouch and handed them to Asin. She carefully took them from Rob, staring at the pair carefully before she nodded and slipped them into her own pouch. Asin was so focused on the stones that she missed the pursing of Rob's lips as she stared at the magical objects.

Tula tapped her foot on the ground, the slight noise and motion causing the experienced Adventurers to look over. The woman nodded to the next walkway, before looking expectantly at the others. At their frowns, she pointed to Asin and then the walkway before staring again.

"Oh," Omrak said, loudly proclaiming his sudden enlightenment. "The woman desires us to continue!"

Tula winced at the loud Northerner, shooting the blond giant a glare who smiled obliviously. Daniel winced, catching the byplay, but waved Asin forwards. The Catkin nodded with a sniff and loped over to the next walkway, bending quickly to scan for danger before proceeding forwards at a markedly faster pace than Tula.

Grinning, Omrak followed after Asin after giving her sufficient space in front. The pair of newcomers glanced at one another, sharing a brief second of camaraderie before they too followed, leaving Daniel to follow behind and muse about the new party mix.

***

Hours later, the quintet finally found the Floor Champion. Or, in their case, the Imp Overseer found them. A floating walkway a few platforms behind them had connected with their route, creating a sudden and entirely unexpected path to the Adventurers. Descending from a platform above the group, through the newly created walkway, the Floor Champion came from behind, his intimidating, muscular but luckily, grounded presence noted by Daniel before the group was surprised. Still, caught out of position, the Adventurers scrambled to adjust their formation.

Daniel sighted down his rockbow, barely able to send a single shot into the incoming group of Imps which preceded the Floor Champion. Behind him, Tula sent arrow after arrow at the group, reserving her Arrow Storm until the Imps were nearly upon the three at the back and releasing the phantom arrows in a wide barrage. The attack caught many of the Imps by surprise, slaying a few and disrupting others, leaving them prey to Rob's spikes.

Rob hid behind Daniel's larger bulk, crouching low behind the armored Adventurer as he withdrew additional enchanted items from his pouches. Ignoring the smaller Imps, Rob rolled a small ball ahead of the group towards the oncoming Floor Champion. The ball bounced over an unseen rock, nearly dropping off the edge of the walkway before coming to a stop, the black and iron patterned steel ball gleaming in the fitful blue light of dungeon's illumination.

"Erlis's tears, that was close," Rob muttered to himself.

Rob then fished out a second, smaller ball and tossed it forwards after whispering a quick incantation. This ball rolled forwards and deployed after three seconds, exploding in a tiny puff of metal. The shattered iron pieces rapidly began to grow icicles on the ground, spiked and frozen caltrops suddenly appearing on the walkway.

By this time, the majority of the remaining Imps had flown past the group, leaving behind minor cuts and bruises. The out of position Imps now flapped their wings as they attempted to gain height or ducked beneath the walkway to approach the group again. Rather than offer the Imps a respite and the chance to attack at their leisure, Omrak roared, triggering his Skill - the Challenge of the North. The Imps, enraged and drawn by the powerful taunt, stopped angling for position and winged towards Omrak, intent on ending the Northerner immediately.

Many of those who approached were batted aside, others were pierced by throwing knives cast by Asin as she loped forwards to aid Omrak. With so many attackers on hand, Asin triggered her own multi-weapon ability, Fan of Knives, creating a spray of throwing weapons that delivered shocking results.

"These are ours, Friend Daniel!" Omrak roared, swinging his giant two-handed sword around, his arms beginning to bleed from small cuts. As he accumulated additional injuries, Omrak's rage Skill activated and a slowly increasing red glow surrounded his body.

"Got it!" Daniel called back, answering Omrak without turning around.

As the large Overseer passed the first of Rob's balls, the enchanted trap exploded into action. It unleashed a cloud of tiny spores into the air which the Overseer inhaled. An errant gust of wind brought some of the spores towards the trio, catching Daniel and Tula by surprise. Both managed to stop themselves from inhaling the spores, but almost immediately Daniel's eyes began to water and itch.

"Close your… oh, nevermind," Rob said, having realised what was happening too late. The Enchanter himself had a pair of newly donned goggles covering his own visage.

With a snarl, Daniel cast **Healer's Mark** on himself and then Tula, grateful that the Overseer, in his sudden partial blindness and coughing fit, had stumbled into the caltrop field. As the healing pulse from the spell took effect, Daniel found his eyes itching and watering less. Still, the delay in casting both spells allowed the Overseer to limp close, it's whip swirling around his body to attack.

Rob, seeing his party mates distracted, gestured with his hands, taking direct control of his enchanted weaponry. The spikes flew downwards, one was batted aside by the whip but diverted its trajectory enough to allow Daniel to catch it on his shield. The second shot forwards towards the Overseer, only to be dodged by a tilt of the Overseer's large body.

"Ba'al's blessing!" Daniel cursed as he dropped the rockbow to the ground and tugged his hammer free. He took a step forwards and then stopped, realising he dared not approach the Overseer across the trapped ground.

"Right," Tula cautioned, her eyes squinted tightly as she loosed an arrow from her recurve bow directly at the Overseer. The arrow gleamed with blue light as the Ranger used her Skill, Penetrating Strike, causing the arrow to fly too fast to be dodged entirely and impaling the Overseer's left shoulder.

With Daniel holding the edge of the trapped zone with his shield and both Rob and Tula harassing the Overseer from a distance, the Floor Boss was forced to duck and dodge attacks in a confined space. Unable to build up momentum across the trapped floor, the Floor Boss was unable to push past Daniel's shield and hammer, suffering from the occasional buzzing strikes of the spikes and the arced **Homing Arrow** shots of Tula that impacted its back. With no recourse, and having had experience fighting the monster before, the group of Adventurers quickly slew the Floor Champion, leaving Asin to pick up the leftover Mana stone and later on, the Floor Chest they found on its original platform.

Their short-term task completed, the group trooped towards the nearest exit – in this case, the entrance towards the second floor and the portal back to the exit at the second floor's entrance. As they traversed back, Daniel could not help but consider the words he would have to speak to his new party members later.

Chapter 2

"That was not a complete disaster," Daniel said to the group as they gathered around their table in the Lonely Candle. A platter of bread had been laid out for the group to eat with a late autumn compote of raspberries and direberries. "For our first run, we cleared the floor - which was great."

"A minimum level of competence I would expect," Rob rebutted with a sniff. "I nearly lost a spike on that last battle."

"Come on, Rob." A friendly elbow struck the Mage's side as Tula smiled at the group. "It wasn't that bad. And it was you who poisoned us."

"And distracted the Overseer!"

"Yes. At least you didn't bring swarms of Imps on us by being too loud," Tula said with a roll of her eyes.

"It would be bad to attract more Imps," Omrak said agreeably, his loud voice rumbling through the tavern. Having spent the last few months in the inn, none of the regulars even turned their heads at the loud Northerner.

"You," Asin said, prodding Omrak in the side with an extended claw. Omrak hissed, edging away from the sharp pain, having discarded his 'stuffy and overbearing' leather tunic upon leaving the Dungeon.

"Friend Daniel has just exhausted his Mana healing me," Omrak said as he rubbed his arms in reflexive recollection of the damage. "We should not force him to work again."

"And you," Rob pointed at Asin and then Tula. "You both need to speak more."

"Hard!" Asin protested, rubbing her throat.

"Dangerous," Tula said, shaking her head. "In the wild, an errant noise can bring disaster. The wilds are not like the dungeon. There are no floors to keep truly dangerous monsters away."

"But we're not in the wild," Daniel added. "Could you not speak a little more? Not everyone understands Ranger hand signals." In fact, Daniel reflected, none of them did beyond Tula. "It would help us understand what you see."

"Bad training creates bad habits," Tula intoned before she shook her head. "Or at least it's what Min always said. And there's little to speak of in the dungeon. I alerted everyone correctly, yes?"

"Yes," Asin agreed immediately, tail waving around behind her. The Catkin fixed large, green cat eyes on the Mage as she dared him to refute her fact.

"Bah! Adventuring is about more than finding and informing each other of the correct dangers. It is about creating a party; a group of fellow teammates one can rely upon. Like the Seven!" Rob said. "How are we to develop such bonds in silence?"

"We don't," Tula said. "I'm here under orders. No one knows what the environment in Artos is going to be like this time. My Skills and training are best served outside of Dungeons, and I'll be there faster than Hursa exiting a bank once this is over."

Daniel snorted at Tula's words, the young God's penchant for thievery a well-known fact.

Hursa rarely being invoked by the majority of Brad had more to do with a desire to avoid his fickle attention, leaving worship of the god extremely sparse. Though, Daniel recalled how the merchants they had escorted discussed how certain villages held to the old ways, providing offerings for all eight of the gods.

"Enchanter Rob is correct. We must work together. For one or more dungeons, our task is not easy as Adventurers," Omrak said. "Trust is important among axe-brothers. But bloodshed is the greatest bind of all."

"Talking of trust," Tula said, eyeing Asin next. "What's with giving Asin all the stones? Don't trust us to hand in our portions properly?"

"No."

"No what?" Rob said, exasperated as he thumped the mug of beer he had just picked up onto the table. "No, you don't trust us or no, you do trust us!"

"Yes," Asin said. Daniel's lips twitched as he noticed how the Catkin's tail swished behind her, her ears flicking back and forth.

"You..."

"What Asin is saying is that we trust you. It's just, well, it's how we do things. Asin is very good at haggling with the merchants when we need to sell the drops outside of the Guild and has the contacts. And rather than having all of us go to the Guild on bad days," Daniel cut in before things grew any worse, "the haggling is something she enjoys doing, and it allows the rest of us time to do our own thing."

"Like what?"

"I train," Omrak said, tapping his chest. "Or visit the docks – though Silverstone has none of those – to earn more coin. Daniel spends his time healing the poor."

"Do-gooder," Tula said with a smirk. But there was a hint of admiration in her voice too.

"Not, well. It's good practice for my skills," Daniel said and then hid behind a hastily raised mug.

"Well, I do not think…" Rob stopped as he was interrupted by Elise, the Innkeeper, arriving with their meal. She began dropping plates in front of the Adventurers, offering both Omrak and Asin a double-portion of the lamb haunch. Once Elise had confirmed the table required no additions, she left. But not before shooting Daniel a worried glance which the Adventurer missed entirely.

"Ahem," Rob said. When he found that none of the others were paying attention to him, he repeated himself louder. When the other somewhat annoyed and hungry team members stared at him, Rob nodded. "We were speaking of the allocation of the Mana stones."

"Oh, leave it be! If we lose Asin's body, we'll probably have bigger problems anyway," Tula said with a wave of her knife. She then ducked her head back down, focusing on her food and sneaking sidelong glances at Omrak and his heaped plate beside her.

"But…"

"I think you're out-voted here, Rob," Daniel said. "We've yet to lose Asin – or the Mana Stones – in all the time we've adventured. I doubt we're about to start."

Rob huffed but fell silent, picking at his food. He stayed in sulky silence for the rest of the mostly silent meal, the hungry Adventurers devouring their plates. It was when everyone had pushed aside their plates that Daniel looked around and spoke slowly.

"So. Omrak's noisy – he'll work on it. Tula and Asin need to communicate a little more for Rob and everyone else's peace of mind. Maybe we can learn some of the more common Ranger signs?" Daniel said and when Tula nodded, he nodded back. "And Rob will be clearer on the kind of enchantments he'll deploy and their effects.

"Did I miss anything?"

"I heard no corrections for yourself, Friend Daniel," Omrak said. "I would wish to hear those from our esteemed colleagues before we end this discussion."

Tula glanced at Rob and then at the rest of the group before raising both of her hands upwards. "No real complaints about Daniel. I've never worked with a Healer before though, so I'm not particularly experienced here. He's not the best fighter I've ever met, but he's not horrid."

"I have. Worked with a healer that is," Rob said, straightening slightly and puffing out his chest. "A number of times actually. Daniel's methods are a departure from the Priest and Herbalist that I'd delved with before. Neither took to the front lines."

"Well, we don't have enough people for me to avoid that," Daniel justified.

"And why is that?" Rob said with a sniff. "There is no reason not to hire a sixth. Certainly, locating another melee fighter would be simple. Those kinds are a dime a dozen."

"Split low," Asin growled.

"Is that why you've been running with three?" Tula asked curiously.

"Not only that," Daniel said, ducking his head low. However, the real reason – that they needed to keep his Gift secret – was not something they were willing to trust their new teammates with. Not yet. "As you've realised, it takes a bit to organise a team."

"The way you work, certainly," Rob said with a nod. "Not all teams are as methodical."

"It's allowed us to clear the Dungeons," Daniel said, frowning slightly.

"Beginner Dungeons. Advanced Dungeons, as you've realised, require a wider range of individuals. If nothing more than to deal with the larger number of monsters. And the Floor Bosses."

Daniel nodded, knowing that their speed of advance, even today with the new members, had been faster than the three of them had experienced before. Of course, thus far, the pair had yet to really take advantage of his abilities as a Healer — the ability to keep entering a Dungeon day-in and day-out. Teams with a Healer had the advantage of in-house help, reducing the team's cost and increasing their ability to arm themselves with better weaponry and armor as well as allowing a constant grind. Many of the Adventuring groups that Rob mentioned had a large number of team members to deal with the lack of Healers — allowing them to rotate in members to keep the team Adventuring.

"Well, I'm not moving to the back lines," Daniel finally decided to state, deciding to make his view clear. Rob's lips tightened but the Enchanter finally nodded, accepting Daniel's statement. "Now, if there's…"

"Finally, back from stealing another place?" Gerardo called as the portly Adventurer stomped over, his sword sheathed by his side and dark eyes flashing with anger. Behind him, Farhad, the dual-wielding fighter, strode behind, olive eyes tight with anger as his robes flowed behind him.

"Stole? We stole nothing!" Tula said angrily, standing.

"Oh, you don't think so? Where do you think your place in Artos came from?" growled out Gerardo.

"Now, Gerardo, that's not exactly fair," Rita called, popping up next to the quintet as she finished quaffing from Asin's mug. "The Guild Master promised that we'd have a chance to enter if a third slot opened up." Her voice was laced with good-natured sarcasm as she spoke. "So, they didn't steal our place, they just dislocated us."

"I…" Daniel stuttered to a stop, realisation crashing down on where their slot had come from. "I didn't know…"

"Of course not. Just because you're a Healer." Gerardo spat to the side. The moment he finished letting the gob of spit loose, Erin appeared next to him, hands on her hips.

"And that's enough of that. Out!"

"You…"

"You spat in my inn, Orange. Get out," Erin growled. The Bloody Blades were only an Orange-ranked team, same as Daniel's team. Just a step above the bare bones Red teams.

"This has nothing…"

"I said out! Your **invitation is revoked**!" Erin snapped. Gerardo's eyes widened as he was suddenly picked up and flung out of the inn, the doors opening up for the Adventurer by themselves as his body flew through the air under its own power. "The rest of you will mind your manners. Or you can leave."

The other pair of Adventurers from the Bloody Blades stared at the quintet before sniffing and walking out after their leader. Daniel winced and opened his mouth and then shut it, realising that the trio had the right of it. While unintentional, it was obvious the Guild Master had made this decision, over-ruling even the Arena results, and creating a new set of enemies for their team.

Yet, Daniel guiltily thought, he would not offer the slot back. Artos was supposed to be a huge Dungeon, and clearing it was important — both for their reputation and their purse.

"Well, that could have gone better," Rob said as he eyed the room that were now watching their table with slight hostility.

"Yeah…" Tula muttered, ducking her head down as if she was attempting to shrink into her chair.

"Tomorrow," Asin said firmly, seeming to ignore the group.

"We should speak with the Guild," Omrak rumbled, taking Asin's lead. "We require training to work as a team further. And perhaps additional equipment."

"Not a horrible idea. I could do with a break from the Dungeon," Rob said, nodding.

"Oh, we're going in if we can," Daniel corrected Rob, watching the Enchanter wince at that pronouncement. "But that'll depend on how hard they train us."

At those words, Rob winced even more.

***

The trip to the large, sprawling two-entranced Adventurers Guild that dominated the centre of the city was not long. As one of the main focus points in the city, there were at least four main streets that approached the building and a half-dozen more that lead close by to it. Unlike Karlak, the small Adventuring town the trio had begun their careers in, Silverstone did have other important industries other than the Dungeons. But still, it was without doubt that the Adventurers Guild held great importance to the city and its economy. Just the streets that led up to the building gave ample evidence of this fact as shopkeepers hawked their wares to the passing Adventurers.

"No, Omrak," Daniel said, gripping the giant Adventurer's elbow gently and tugging with force, dragging the Northerner away from a roadside stand. "We're not stopping for you to shop."

"But the powder they offer will provide an increase in heat resistance!" Omrak argued.

"Crushed Juha leaves are the main component of those bags," Rob said as he walked beside the pair. "An obvious alchemical mixture."

"Juha leaves?"

"They're a plant, most commonly found in the Eastern marshes," Daniel said. "You can buy the leaves, whole, for about two copper a bag. And still get a decent amount of the heat resistance effects. Very useful for those suffering from heatstroke."

"Then…"

"It does nothing to stop burn damage," Rob said with a roll of his eyes. "Heat resistance does not equate to burn resistance. One affects your ability to handle high temperatures. The other is sudden, painful and scarring."

"That's not how the comparison works," Tula piped up from their side. Daniel absently noted how the Ranger had chosen to take the middle of the group, staying away from the edges of the crowd as they walked.

"It is good enough for our barbarian companion," Rob replied.

"But why would anyone sell such an item if it had no use in the upcoming Dungeons?" Omrak complained plaintively.

"The same reason they sold you the 'enchanted' trap finders, the 'flask of never-ending wine' and that cursed, knotted rope," Daniel said. "Because you have money and they want it."

"The flask *is* never-ending," Omrak protested.

"With wine so bad we use it as vinegar," Daniel added. "And it pours out at a rate of a cup an hour. It's a good thing that Erin allowed us to trade it in for your month's rent."

Omrak grimaced but nodded, falling silent. Still, it took all but ten minutes before the blond giant spotted another deal. This time though, even Daniel found himself intrigued as he stared at the half-dozen rings that gleamed under the glass container.

"Rings of water breathing," Daniel read out loud for Omrak. His friend was still working on learning his words, and so, in cases like this, Daniel was more than happy to help the youngster. "And a decent price for enchanted equipment too."

"You've got a good eye," the merchant said as he came out of the shop, stroking his long beard and smiling wide. "I am selling all these rings as a set."

"A set?" Daniel frowned and eyed the price. Just over thirty gold for the set of six rings. Which placed each ring at five gold each? Considering the enchanted bracers that he had once commissioned had cost twelve gold – and that was at cost of materials – these rings were a bargain. In fact, almost too much of a bargain.

"Too cheap," Asin butted in and pointed at the rings. "Why?"

The shopkeeper's lips pressed tightly for the briefest of moments when he spotted the Beastkin. But as a shopkeeper that targeted Adventurers, he surpassed his own prejudice quickly and answered Asin. "There is nothing wrong with the rings if you that is what you believe. They are just somewhat specific in their requirements."

"Yes?"

"Well, the rings…"

"Must be used in conjunction," Rob interrupted. "They are useless alone. The Enchanter was likely attempting to cut costs when enchanting and used a single ritual circle, one that he did not alter to accommodate multiple rings. As such, the ritual linked each of the rings."

"Who are you?" the shopkeeper said, frowning at Rob. "How did you know that?"

"A simple deduction from viewing the ritual glyphs," Rob replied with a sniff. "The rings are not even worth the cost of their base materials. Which were sub-par."

"Sub-par!" the shopkeeper hissed in affront and pointed with his fingers. "Leave. These rings are not for you. And you can forget about shopping at my store again. Any of you!"

"But…" Daniel began to protest but the shopkeeper sniffed, turning away from the Adventurer. Daniel frowned but eventually gave up, walking away whilst shooting a miffed look at Rob. The Enchanter just shrugged his shoulders while Asin just shook her head behind the pair, her tail lashing as they finally made their way to the Guild, pushing their way through the crowds.

Chapter 3

The Adventurers Guild was a large building that sat raised above the surrounding buildings with a series of wide stairs leading to the off-white building and the entrance doors. The building itself consisted of two main entrances, the Adventurers which travelled to each entrance distinct in form and manner. Questors took the one nearest the group - individuals who focused on completing requests from the general populace. Tula, as a Ranger, would be highly familiar with that section. In the other entrance, the 'true' work of Adventurers lay and where the Delvers entered, picking up Dungeon specific notices and quests or just turning in Dungeon loot. While it was possible to sell Dungeon loot outside of the Guild, the only legal location to sell Mana stones was at the Guild. No surprise then that most Adventurers took the slight loss for the greater convenience of selling everything at the same location.

Trudging up the stairs, the group entered the second entranceway. Daniel paid slight attention to the notification board, curious to see if there were any additional updates on the Dungeons. He immediately dismissed notes about Aramis, having insufficient time or context to understand the details, and focused on updates for Porthos. Seeing nothing new, he sped up. Meanwhile, behind him, Asin and Rob were eying the displayed prices for the Mana stones and Dungeon loot while Tula and Omrak just watched the people.

The quintet drew mild attention on their entrance. The addition of the Selkie - in Rob - the

Catkin and the giant Omrak made their group somewhat unique, especially with the fame that the team had garnered through the arena fights. Yet, to Daniel's surprise, he noted that none of the guild members approached them. In fact…

"We've not been approached at all. By other guilds," Daniel clarified to his friends.

"Did you not know? The Guild Master has requested that the team not be disturbed before our entrance to Artos," Tula said, chiming in. "Not that I would change guilds," she added, tapping the small emblem of a curling ivy stick that was sewn onto the chest of her tunic.

"What guild is that?" Omrak asked, pointing to Tula's emblem.

"The Western Ivy," Tula replied. "It mostly consists of Rangers, Scouts and Explorers. We're mostly Questors by choice more than need. But try explaining that to your average guild." Tula rolled her eyes. "Nooo… we all have to clear the Dungeons to be considered a 'real' Adventurer."

Asin frowned, cocking her head to the side at Tula's bitching before she slunk closer. "Leave?"

"And go where? We still need enchanted equipment and Mana stones. Cheapest way to get both is to be part of the Adventurers Guild," Tula said with a sniff. "And it's not as if it's not been tried before. But everyone's used to giving their quests to the Guild."

Daniel nodded as Tula expounded on another aspect of the world he'd yet to encounter. As they finished the conversation, with Tula continuing to complain about the guilds and the Guild, they exited the back of the building where the training grounds were located.

It was there that they found Seth, the Beastkin turtle that manned the main training desk, lounging under the awning and watching his domain with half-lidded eyes. The Turtlekin grinned as the group approached, and he sat upwards, cocking his head from side-to-side as he spotted the additions to the party.

"I see you finally decided to arrive!" he said as he pulled out three yellow slips and pushed them forwards on his table. "You three, give back your orange sheaths."

Daniel paused for a second, and while he hesitated, his friends strode past him to take hold of the sheaths, extracting their own Adventurer Cards from their inventory and replacing the simple sheaths. Daniel followed suit soon afterwards, preening slightly until he realised that both of his new companions had Green sheaths on the cards they showed to Seth when the conversation turned to the actual reason for their trip here.

"Team tactics?" Seth rubbed his chin in thought. "I'm assuming you want tactics you can learn and use in Artos?" At the almost simultaneous nods the group offered him, Seth grinned. "Well, I've got just the trainer for you, but you aren't going to like it."

"It's Angie isn't it."

"It's Angie."

Daniel groaned, having his voiced premonition made true. It was not as if he disliked the older, one-eyed muscular trainer. It was just that he understood how brutal her training methods were. Still, he could see how the experienced Adventurer would be perfect for their needs. None of the other trainers would push them hard enough to actually ingrain the tactics they needed.

"How much?"

"You want her for the week?" Seth asked.

"Do we?" Daniel turned to the group, unsure exactly how much they needed an actual trainer and how much of the tactics they provided they could then use in the Dungeon. After all, training was good, but there was nothing like the pressure of actual application to make things click. Or show the flaws in their applications.

Seth rapped the table, dragging Daniel's attention back as the group hummed and hawed, debating the various merits of booking a trainer for the entire period and breaking up their training periods. With their attention drawn back to him, Seth smiled.

"Why don't I make it easier for you? The Guild Master has indicated he'll subsidize your training if you were smart enough to come. So, for a Gold each, you can train with Angie as much as you need for the week," Seth said. He looked right at Daniel as he said that, offering the Healer a meaningful look. When Daniel just stared back blankly at the Turtlekin, Seth continued. "*Angie* will get full payment for her time for the week, of course. All of it. For all of you."

"Oh," Daniel brightened up as he got the hint. Of course. Angie was always short of funds, having a slight drinking problem and a larger personality one. Her abrasive personality and her harsh training methods meant few Adventurers willingly worked with the experienced Adventurer. "Here's my Gold."

"I do feel it should be a group decision," Rob grumbled but then fished out a gold piece too. "But it is a great deal."

Omrak, of course, just handed his payment over without a word as did Asin. Though the Catkin did so with a slight wince. It left Tula standing there alone, staring at the group.

"Tula?"

"We could save more," Tula said, frowning. "I'm not convinced this is a good use of our funds."

"Angie's very good. Seth said so," Daniel pointed to the Turtlekin, "and he's not led us wrong."

"Still, we should perhaps look at our other options first..."

"And spend hours interviewing everyone?" Daniel shook his head and pointed at the four. "We've already paid. You're out-voted, I think."

Tula stared at the Healer and then around the group before her lips pursed tight. She drew and tossed the gold coin to Seth, muttering softly under her breath.

"This is why I hate groups."

Acting as if he did not hear her words, Daniel took the training chit from Seth gratefully and headed for the training grounds. Time to find their trainer.

***

They found Angie easily, the fortyish older Adventurer was leaning against one of the wooden posts that fenced off the training grounds, watching a pair of experienced Adventurers pound on each other with dual-wielding maces. Her single eye gleamed, sweat from the sun's heat showcasing the bronzed and muscular skin under her simple leather tunic.

"Angie?" Daniel called out as they neared. Angie turned and grinned as she saw Daniel, waving to him and abandoning her post. The fighters did not seem to mind, continuing their sparring match without pause.

"Daniel. Back for more?" Angie said as she eyed the chit in his hand. Daniel just chuckled and tossed the chit to the Adventurer who fumbled the catch and dropped it. As she bent to pick up the chit, she pocketed it and shot forward, catching Daniel around both his legs with surprise and taking him to the ground. His friends dispersed quickly, though Daniel caught the edge of Rob's shin as he went down.

"Owwww!" Daniel groaned. Still, Angie did not keep him down, instead getting off him and backing off with a smirk. "What was that for?" Daniel said with a groan as he pushed himself to a seated position.

"I've only got one eye, idiot," Angie said good-naturedly. Daniel winced, realising that her depth perception was probably significantly off. Still…

"You didn't have to be that hard," Daniel grumbled as he stood up.

"If you had kept up your training, you'd have dodged me," Angie countered.

"Ahem. We're here for another reason," Rob said, interrupting the pair. Daniel shot the Enchanter a look before he turned to the expectant Angie.

"We're hiring you for the week to help us with our team tactics. This is Rob Keeton, an Enchanter, and Tula Perron, a Ranger. They're joining us for our trip to Artos." Daniel waved to the pair in turn as he spoke. "We need to add them to our normal formations and were told you would be able to help us develop tactics that would suit us."

"Sure. But I'm going to need a little more information," Angie said and waved the group to where a set of benches awaited. Most of the group had started moving there, leaving only Tula who hesitated before raising her hand slightly.

"Yes?" Angie said when she turned around to see what was taking the Ranger so long.

"Don't you have another session?" Tula pointed to the still-sparring pair.

"Nah. You're more interesting," Angie said. When she spotted the grimace on Tula's face, Angie laughed slightly and added, "They also didn't pay me. I was just doing it because I was bored."

"Oh..." Tula nodded and followed along afterwards. What she thought of that revelation, she kept to herself.

"So, why don't you tell me about your Skills. I know the original DAO's but perhaps we should go over it again, just in case," Angie said.

Taking turns, the group began to list their Skills. This was the second time they were doing so in short order, but none of the team hesitated in doing so. In particular, the group listed both their major combat skills and their relevant Skills to Angie. On the other hand, Daniel wondered if any were holding back – certainly, he was in not detailing his Gift.

"Alright, so here's what we have. At the longest range, only Tula is effective. At short-mid range, you have a limited amount of ranged attacks between Asin and Omrak. At melee range, nearly all of you are effective to some extent - except for Tula whose preferred weapon becomes less useful. That's not including your Enchanter of course. He's rather useless and useful at the same time," Angie said with a grimace. "He has a very limited amount of combat skills, but a large variety of utility enchanted items and a few useful utility spells. Overall, I'd plan for him to stay in the middle and act as the reserve, helping those who need it. He's more useful there than actively engaging.

"That sound about right to you all?"

Daniel pursed his lips, thinking over what Angie said. For once, even Rob was silent while the Adventurers considered her words. In the end, after receiving their reluctant agreement, Angie continued. "Good. In that case, what we'll do is work you all through a series of formations from long to close range encounters. We'll set you up in your basic formation, have you work basic tactical guidelines in each, and then alter your formation to deal with different situations and have you work those tactics again. It won't be exact movements, but at least you'll all be working from the same guidelines."

"Guidelines?" Rob said with a frown.

"Guidelines. They differ with each group. A scout-based group with more ranged attacks would attempt to hit and disperse, bleeding their attackers. Daniel's group, before your addition, mostly took ranged attacks of opportunity but would focus on closing the distance on ranged attackers quickly. For now, with Tula, you're in a somewhat more traditional party with a mix of ranged and melee fighters, with an emphasis – as always – on melee. But as Omrak is without a shield, you won't be able to hide and shoot, so you're better off staying aggressive," Angie explained. "Overall, your tactics won't change much from what DAO had previously – take ranged attacks when possible, close in on ranged fighters when not. But there is going to be an emphasis on a higher level of defense.

"But words mean little. Let's hit the field and I'll show you what I mean."

***

Hours later, the team lay on the ground or hung off the fences of the arenas, breathing deeply and groaning. Asin snorted slightly as Omrak nursed a sore shoulder, refusing to mention the injury to Daniel even though the Catkin had distinctly heard the muffled groan when Angie's hip threw him to the ground. Not that any of the others were doing much better, including herself, the Beastkin considered. Together with the other inactive and bored trainers, Angie had repeatedly drilled the team in the group movements needed to coordinate around one another. And then, she beat the lessons into their bodies.

Unlike the others, Asin had done well. It helped that both her Cat's Intuition and Greater Agility Skills provided her with an almost unfair advantage. With her Intuition and expanded senses, she knew where everyone was and could guess where they would go. And when that failed, she could dodge around their inappropriately located bodies. That did not help when her teammates made their way into the path of her knives, but as it was Daniel and Omrak who fought in-close, those issues rarely occurred.

Unfortunately, none of Asin's advantages stopped the newcomers from blundering into the wrong areas or failing to provide the right kind of help when needed. Tula often found herself out of position, unable to support the group with cover fire without risking hitting her teammates, while Rob was even more useless. At the least, at times, Tula could enter melee range to aid the team. Rob, with his limited arsenal of abilities and lower intuitive sense for the flow of combat, was often utterly useless or worse - a danger to the group.

"Daniel, you need to learn patience," Angie said as she pointed at the bruised and battered healer. "Your strength and Skills are not keeping up with the new dungeon monsters you're facing as you transition to a healer role. While your armor keeps you safe, it will not do so if you overextend yourself. Stop rushing the kill and trust your companions to survive. And heal them if they don't." Daniel nodded sullenly, his scent bringing the acrid smell of resentment briefly to Asin's nose before the Adventurer brought his feelings under control. Once again, Asin found herself admiring how controlled her friend could be – it was a maturity that belied his age.

"Omrak, you need to learn to stop pushing forwards. You are the linchpin of the forward formation. If you step forwards too far, you break the line and allow us to step around you and attack your team. Worse, you have ranged attackers behind you. Unlike Asin, they do not know you and until they do, you put yourself in danger from their attacks with your actions," Angie continued. "Fix it."

"Yes, Honored Teacher," Omrak said. Asin sniffed slightly, taking in the smell of Omrak. Young, full of vigor and hormones. Eager still, even after the repeated bruising and damage. But underneath all that, a thread of sourness from suppressed pain. Asin growled mentally, knowing that Omrak was likely hiding a more significant injury from Daniel. She would need to inform Daniel. Thus far, the innocent and naïve Omrak had yet to realise it was Asin who tattled on his attempts to hide his injuries.

"Rob. You need to pay attention to the flow of battle more and control your spikes. I think you should only use a single spike for attacks for now.

Keep the second for defense. Your Magic Arrow – whether Mana or Ice enhanced – is powerful, but should be used sparingly. And don't use your poison without confirmation."

Rob's lips twisted and his back straightened, anger tickling Asin's nose as the Enchanter had a strip torn into his ego. But he stayed silent, which was an improvement over the start of their training.

"Asin – stop relying on your Skills. You're not memorising the tactics or where your teammates are going to be. You're relying on your ability to read their movements," Angie continued turning to the Catkin. "That works, until it doesn't. You don't have time to learn each other's motivations normally, so you have to rely on the tactics." Asin bobbed her head in acknowledgement, but Angie was already turning to their last member, staring straight at Tula. "As for you, Ranger, you need to grow more confident. Take the shots that the team gives you."

"But they're moving…"

"Then that's their problem. Especially the big guy. He won't learn without a few arrows in him," Angie said and pointed at Daniel. "You're on a team with a Healer. Use it."

Asin nodded at the words, tail lashing out behind her. It was all good advice, but receiving advice and putting it into practice were two different things entirely. Before any of the team could say anything, Angie pointed to the exit of the training grounds and added. "Good. Now, get yourself watered, fed and into the Dungeon. We've done enough talking and practising."

"Is that wise?" Daniel said with a frown and Angie shrugged.

"Is dungeoning wise? Is sending an Orange team into a newly opened Dungeon smart?" Angie said with a smirk. "You take risks if you want the rewards. And you can't afford to not clear that Dungeon."

The group grimaced but nodded, Asin feeling her tail swish around behind her. Another sniff brought the scent of a new determination to her. Even if Angie was not particularly eloquent, her point had been made. They were Adventurers. Their job was to take risks. Even if they were greater than normal.

Chapter 4

Daniel sighed as he looked around the grouped parties in front of the Adventuring Guild. A week later, and after numerous arduous training sessions, the team had come together. While the tactics they had worked out and trained with Angie were still rough, the gruelling hours of training had seen a significant improvement in their teamwork. No longer did Rob throw his enchanted balls of poison around without warning the group. Tula, with her greater archery skills, could now support the team even when the monsters neared them. And, perhaps most surprisingly to Daniel, Omrak had managed to learn to not charge ahead at every instance.

Standing in the morning sunlight, Daniel peered at the numerous teams that would join them in delving Artos. While every single one of these Adventuring parties were Advanced Adventurers like them, all of them were ranked higher. The highest ranked teams were violet ranked, teams who were on the cusp of becoming Master Adventurers and thus able to enter the most dangerous Dungeons on Brad. And, Daniel reflected, it showed in their bearing and equipment. Each of the violet teams bore at least a trio of enchanted items, many wielding enchanted weapons and defensive equipment. Those, due to their size and importance, were much more expensive than basic enchanted items.

"The Flying Tigers, the Troll Killers, the Eight," Omrak muttered to Tula, the pair happily gossiping about the various groups with wide-eyed wonder. "Such a large collection of Heroes. Did you know, the Troll Killers gained their name from their very first Quest?"

Daniel found himself smiling slightly, regarding his teammates fondly. The group had gelled well, but this was the first time he had seen everyone in a day. Rather than push themselves too hard, the group had taken the last day off after a healing session with him. Now, equipment buffed and fixed, everyone looked eager to enter Artos. Daniel briefly wondered what everyone had done - though from the smug look on Asin's face and the quick nuzzling of faces he had noted of Asin and Tevik, he had a guess, at least, of the Catkin's activities yesterday.

As for himself, Daniel had spent the day working at a nearby free clinic, helping to heal those who could not afford it. His sessions at the clinic were quite popular, even if they were irregular. He still felt uncomfortable with how so many regarded his acts as entirely altruistic. In reality, he used his time at the clinic to help progress his own skills – a necessary requirement for upgrading his own Healing spells. Of course, he could have done the same while charging for his services, but it was a factor that he refused to consider too greatly.

It was in the evening when Daniel finally found time to upgrade his Level. With a flick of his mind, Daniel called up his character sheet once again.

Name: Daniel Chai (Advanced Rank Adventurer)
Race: Human (Male)
Class: Level 11 Adventurer (21%)
Sub-classes: Level 7 (Miner) (2.5%)
Life: 311
Stamina: 311
Mana: 229

Attributes

Strength: 29
Agility: 25
Constitution: 31
Intelligence: 24
Willpower: 20
Luck: 16

Skills

Unarmed Combat: Level 8 (47/100)
Clubs (Novice): Level 7 (02/100)
Archery: Level 3 (04/100)
Shield (Novice): Level 6 (82/100)
Dodge (Novice): Level 1 (57/100)
Combat Sense (Novice): Level 4 (63/100)
Perception (Novice): Level 3 (11/100)
Mining: Level 7 (78/100)
Healing (Novice): Level 4 (08/100)
Herb Lore: Level 3 (48/100)
Stealth: Level 2 (34/100)
Cooking: Level 4 (13/100)
Singing: Level 2 (14/100)
Tactics: Level 3 (02/100)

Skill Proficiencies

Double Strike	Shield Bash
Perin's Blow	Find Weakness
Mapping (II)	Inventory
	(Adventurer Special)

Spells

Minor Healing (II)	Healer's Mark (I)

Gifts

Martyr's Touch—The caster may heal oneself or others by touch and concentration, sacrificing a portion of his life to do so. Cost varies depending on the extent of the injuries healed.

While his Level had not increased, Daniel was particularly happy about the increases in his skills. Forced to understand where his team would go and the tactics employed, he found that he had significantly increased his Combat Sense and Perception skills as well as acquiring a base Tactics skill. On top of that, his new goal of hunkering behind his shield had increased his skill with the defensive equipment even further, providing him with a nice boost. In fact, Daniel looked forward to seeing what kind of new Skills he might receive due to the recent increases. Find Weakness, as it stood, was a powerful Skill of his which allowed him to turn the tables against stronger, better-armored opponents numerous times.

A rustle and change in mood among the groups drew Daniel's attention back to the team as one final, last-minute addition was added. His lips peeled apart slightly, noting how the Falling Leaves, the Orange team that Daniel had bumped from their spot, were here. A brief glance around and Daniel ascertained that, including the Falling Leaves, his team was the only other Orange team. He had been too awed to notice this fact earlier.

"What's going on?" Daniel muttered. "Why are they here?"

"Other team. Broke up," Asin said. "Sleeping with each other. Drama!"

"Oh yes, it was very interesting gossip. Happened just last night," Rob said, chuckling softly. "It seems their team leader caught the mage and his lover sleeping together. For the sixth time! Declaring he could not 'do this anymore' the team leader stalked out of the city. His lover followed, of course, and the mage scurried back to his own master."

"Really?" Daniel blinked, then remembered that the Blackened Blades had been an all-male team. Not an entirely surprising matter since women made up a smaller number in Adventuring groups. The hardship, the physical requirements and frankly, the wider option of careers available to women made them less likely to take on such a difficult and dangerous career. "Drama indeed."

Daniel sighed, eyeing the Falling Leaves. This did not bode well. While each party going into the Dungeon would be acting by themselves, the teams which were in the Orange or Red groups would be on the lower Levels together. In the event of an emergency, they would have to rely on one another. But with the animosity between the groups, Daniel could not help but dread the idea of asking for help from the other team.

"Now that everyone has gathered, I'd like to say a few words," the Guild Master's voice rang out across the square, dragging the attention of the various Adventuring parties back. Daniel turned to the older man who controlled their careers. "As many of you know, the opening of Artos is unprecedented at this time interval. It is believed the opening is due to an unnatural increase in the number of Dungeon monsters - requiring an active suppression attempt by the teams we are sending in.

"If this is true, it will mean you will be facing greater dangers than any previous team. But Erlis does not endanger without providing reward. It is likely the rewards for what you will face will have also increased. Those who risk will triumph. Those who hide will fade."

All around the square, Adventurers nodded their heads. It was part of their lives, their calling to risk it all for gains. And for the civilians who lived their lives without ever entering a Dungeon. Without them, the corruption that Ba'al had implanted in the world would boil over, sending monsters into the surroundings. It was their job, as

Adventurers, to ensure that Dungeons never broke.

"All of you have received what aid we can provide - including a list of all the monsters that have ever been encountered in Artos as well as maps of the Dungeon. But, as you know, Artos changes each time it opens, and we do not expect this to be any different," the Guild Master said, his eyes sweeping over everyone. "Good luck. And good delving."

At his final pronouncement, the Adventurers echoed their thanks. Daniel touched his belt pouch where a single healing potion sat, a gift from the Adventurers Guild. It was, obviously, not likely to be enough, but in itself, it was a generous act. Healing potions were expensive and rare.

Having finished his pronouncement, the Guild Master turned and left. Soon afterwards, attendants streamed out to meet each Adventuring team to lead them towards the newly opened Dungeon. Together, the group slowly tromped through the crowded streets, filled with farmers heading to market, bakers and other early risers. Yet, upon sight of the Adventurers, the civilians parted to give way to the group, whispered conversations marking their journey.

"It seems even the civilians are aware of the import," Rob said as he glanced at the parting crowd. "It would be a grievous felony if we failed to clear our portion."

"We shall not fail!" Omrak replied. "It is only a few floors after all. And we cleared the second floor of Porthos easily!"

"It is easier with our new friends," Daniel chimed in, nodding to Tula and Rob. Tula just smiled slightly, skirting deeper into the group as the crowd continued to stare at them all, while Rob strode forwards with the side of his mouth curled up in a smile.

In this manner the teams walked, heading north from the Adventurers Guild to finally arrive at a walled-off section of the city. A large gate was swung open, watched over by the town guards who waved the Adventurers in after confirming their presence with the attendants.

Forced to wait outside the enclosure, the team milled about, chatting softly.

"What kind of dungeon do you think it'll be? Another cave or something wilder?" Daniel asked softly.

"I hope it's a forest," Tula said, absently running her fingers over the ends of her arrows. "It'd be nice to be in one again."

"Even if it's artificial?" Daniel said curiously.

"Better than nothing."

"A mountainous Dungeon floor would be good," Omrak chimed in with a grin.

"Not water," Asin said with a low yowl. Even if the group had chipped in and purchased the water breathing rings, it was still not a floor any of them would be comfortable in. Especially the picky Catkin.

"I do not care of the environment, but humanoid monsters would be best," Rob said, touching the small enchanted spheres he carried. "My poisons work best against those."

"Well, I doubt it'll be kobolds," Daniel said with a smile, making his original friends chuckle at shared memories.

"DAO!" the Guild attendant called. The party quickly moved forwards, streaming into the enclosure. The party immediately spotted the single, glowing, double-doored portal that was the entrance to the Dungeon. sIts swirling colours gave no further hint of what might be within.

"You know, I think we should change the party name," Tula said. "After all, we're part of the group now."

"So, you wished to be known as DAROT? Or perhaps TAROD?" Rob said scornfully. "I prefer not."

"Something with a little more flair," Tula rebutted as the group walked towards the Dungeon portal. As Daniel was about to enter it, Omrak reached out and gripped Daniel's arm, shaking his head.

"This is my honor," Omrak said.

"No," Asin said, prodding the Northerner in the side. When Omrak frowned, Asin pointed to the attendant who was busy playing with some stones to the side.

"Ah…" Omrak subsided, waiting for the attendant to finish configuring the portal. As they waited, the Falling Leaves entered as well. The parties fell into an uneasy silence, eyeing each other warily. In the end, Daniel drew a shaky breath and walked over to Gerardo.

"Gerardo, congratulations on getting in. And, well, I hope you do well," Daniel said, offering his hand.

"Only someone like you would wish to gain entry into a Dungeon by such means," Rita said with a snarl. "Take your backstabbing hand out of here. Don't think you're going to convince us to go easy. We'll get the Floor Champion and the Floor Chest for both floors!"

Daniel grimaced slightly at her words, taken aback by the vitriol. When he glanced over to Gerardo, all he saw was the portly Adventurer glaring back at Daniel. Defeated, Daniel slunk back to the team.

"That went well," Rob said sarcastically.

"No," Asin said, her tail lashing out behind her as she glared at Rob and then the other team.

"Fear not, Friend Daniel. We shall show the Fallen Leaves that we deserve our place," Omrak said clapping his friend on the shoulder. When the attendant nodded to the group to indicate the portal was ready, Omrak strode forwards only to be brought up short by Farhad who had slipped ahead of him. The robed and masked swordsman just stared up at the big Northerner as his teammates slipped past. Omrak glared downwards, but a quick shake of Daniel's head stopped the Northerner from acting further.

As the last of the Fallen Leaves walked into the shimmering portal, Tula muttered, "Now I'm getting annoyed. Let's beat their uppity asses."

Daniel could only nod to those words while waiting for the attendant to reconfigure the portal again. In minutes, it was ready, and the party stepped into the Dungeon portal.

Chapter 5

As the first through the portal, Omrak knew his job was to ensure that the area around the entrance was clear. While it was highly unlikely for there to be monsters near the entrance, it was still an important precaution to take. As such, the giant Northerner strode forwards immediately and started looking around, searching for trouble.

The first thing Omrak noticed was that they had exited in an area with significant illumination. In fact, the light source was not the usual slightly blue illumination of Mana-imbued stones but a more natural light source reminiscent of the first level of Porthos. The second thing Omrak noticed was that the mist covered the ground below the hill he was on, ensuring that the lowlands of the moor that splayed out before him were hidden. Only a few higher hills like the one he was on were visible. In the distance, Omrak could just about see the gleam of something that did not look at all natural. Admittedly, natural was a loose term in a Dungeon. The last thing that Omrak discovered was the slight chill that pervaded the Dungeon floor, one that made the Northerner grin.

"Cold!" Asin yelped as she walked in and prowled the edges of the hilltop. Her tail lashed out behind her as she sniffed the air and eyed the grassy flooring.

"A perfect temperature!" Omrak rebutted, stretching wide as he walked to the edge of the hill before it started dropping precipitously down. He laughed, eyeing the rolling mists below for hints of what they might encounter.

"Quiet," Tula growled as she joined Omrak near the edge. The blonde noted how she kept a decent distance from him and stayed further away from his left, allowing him to draw his sheathed, cross-body great sword without hitting her. He found himself nodding in gratitude. Some things, obviously, had been ingrained over the past week's training.

"I am quiet, Hero Tula," Omrak said but lowered his voice to slightly above a whisper nonetheless.

"She's right," Daniel said as he joined the group, eyeing the ground below. "Mists like this generally mean we're looking at ambush predators of some sort. No need to make it easier for them to find us."

"Are we keeping a close or open formation?" Rob asked, frowning at the mists. A hand touched a bracelet on his arm, the only defensive item that the mage carried. Other than the light chainmail jerkin that he wore to cover his body.

"Tula?" Daniel asked the Ranger.

"Closed for now," Tula said after considering the environment one last time. "I don't know this area well enough to scout too far ahead. The monsters might be able to confuse or obfuscate themselves too, so splitting the party would be a bad idea."

"Agreed," Asin said, sniffing the air again before she wrinkled her nose. But she did not comment further so Omrak turned away from the Catkin to Daniel who was staring at the mists.

"Direction?" Daniel asked, squinting as he searched for a clue for the Dungeon exit.

"I see something gleaming in the distance," Tula said, pointing slightly farther to her left.

"Alright then. We'll use the standard close formation. Tula, keep in sight," Daniel commanded. "We'll travel in the direction of what Tula saw. Tula, we'll want to ascend the hills until we know what we're facing. I don't want to be in the mists for too long. Everyone, take a bearing now."

After receiving confirmations from everyone, Omrak took out his compass and gauged the distance and bearing. Of course, the Dungeon compass they were using pointed not to 'North' but to the portal entrance. Still, by fixing a specific direction and taking the direction of where they were to go, in the event of one of the party being split from the others, they would still be able to meet up.

"Everybody good?" Daniel asked one last time. Having received confirming nods, the group walked down the hill, Tula in the lead and Asin at the back.

Omrak turned his head from side to side, scanning the surroundings as they walked forwards. Once they entered the mists fully, his line of sight dropped to barely ten feet, the distance that Tula's shrouded figure held before their group. The Ranger moved through the thick fern-like shrubbery of the moors, her bow held strung down before her, arrows held loosely between her free fingers while she stalked forwards. Omrak could see her head constantly turning, taking in new environmental features, wary of potential problems.

Together the group traipsed through the Dungeon floor, going from one hill to another. Tension slowly rose as the lack of attacks made the group grow more and more nervous. After all, one truism of all Dungeons was that they always contained monsters – corrupted creatures created through the expulsion of Ba'al's taint from Erlis.

It was as they traversed a deep gully towards the third hill that Tula paused, holding a hand up. She swiftly dropped her hand towards her bow, nocking an arrow with her free hand. Too slowly however as the presence she had noticed lunged from behind the giant fern leaves it had hidden behind, bowling the Ranger over.

Omrak roared, instinctively charging forwards. Even as he did so, he noticed additional movement now as other monsters dashed from hiding. Four-foot-tall bipedal monsters with scaly skin, a quartet of hooked claws, and a thin, balancing tail dashed forwards from hiding to launch themselves at the group. Omrak instinctively drew and cut at the monster attacking him, his sword cutting and throwing the monster aside. Behind him, he could hear more monsters arriving.

Quadra Raptor (Level 9)
HP: 138/140

Slowing his footsteps for a second, Omrak raised the sword above his head as he roared out loud, triggering his Skill **Challenge of the North**. Immediately, he could hear the creatures change direction, breaking away from his friends to assault him. Crouching down low, the blade held near his hip and angled backwards, the Northerner waited.

Already, the monster that he had directed most of his attention towards – the one assaulting Tula – had jumped off the woman, clawed feet leaving deep wounds on her body as it left her prone form. A breath before it arrived, Omrak swung, twisting his hips and throwing his front leg backwards, spinning in a circle to cut the monsters both in front of him and those approaching behind. Whether by luck or skill, he managed to injure both Tula's attacker and one of his attackers from behind. Having ended his spin facing opposite from where he had started, Omrak had just about enough time to note that there were three remaining raptors, leaving the attacking party a total of five.

The one that first attacked him was still recovering, a second was still engaged with Daniel and a third had avoided his blow by virtue of being slow. That last one threw itself at Omrak, its clawed feet failing to find purchase on his leather tunic but clawed hands tearing at his upper arms and leaving a minor nick on his neck. With a snarl, Omrak straightened and cut upwards at an angle, ripping open the raptor's chest cavity. Before he could attack it again, the other three raptors were on him and he was forced to wave his sword around to guard against the monsters.

"Line!" Daniel called out, his voice slightly breathless as he charged towards Omrak.

As he fought, Omrak noted the raptor crawling feebly on the ground, a hand crushed and its legs hamstrung while Rob directed a spike to finish it. Near Daniel, Asin rushed to join him, placing herself just slightly behind the armored healer to use her throwing knives to best effect.

Omrak quickly took a step sideways, angling his body as he waited for his friend to arrive. The motion opened up a gap in his weaving defense, allowing a raptor to jump and clamp its serrated, double-rowed set of teeth onto his sword arm. Grunting with the added weight and pain, Omrak staggered, allowing the other raptors a new opening.

Even as the raptors crouched low to jump, an arrow and pair of throwing knives impaled two of the creatures, distracting them. The second raptor was shield-rushed by Daniel, his heavy shield and form bowling over the smaller creature. Stumbling,

Daniel righted himself and swung his hammer around, crushing a rib cage.

"You filthy monster!" Omrak snarled, raising his free hand to plunge his thumb into the slitted eye of the monster still hanging from his arm. In pain, the raptor opened its mouth and fell, allowing Omrak to boot the monster into a nearby fern where it struggled to stand. Just as it got back to its feet, the angry giant swung his sword, beheading the creature.

"They're running!" Rob called, his hand twisting and gesturing as he controlled a magical spike to dart forwards to strike at one of the raptors. True to the Enchanter's words, the surviving raptors were attempting to run. A last arrow by Tula caught a previously feathered monster in the side, hobbling it and allowing Asin to jump on its back and, while gripping its neck with one arm and reaching around to plunge her knife deep into its side before back-flipping off.

"No, you don't," Daniel snarled as he reached the other raptor, swinging his weapon to keep it distracted and focused on him. Unable to finish the monster quickly, Daniel fell back towards his team. With a glance at his friend, Daniel threw up **Healer's Mark** on both Tula and Omrak before the group fell into a tense, watchful silence. In time, the bodies of the raptors around them dispersed into blue motes of light, leaving behind their Mana Stones. Several tense minutes later, the team ascertained that they were not about to be attacked again.

"That could have gone better," Rob said into the silence, eying the damage done to Omrak. Strips of flesh, peeking out from under the hastily wrapped bandages, were torn from the large Northerner's arm. The damage was visibly healing with each pulse of magic, but even then, slow dribbles of blood fell to the ground.

"Omrak, you need to keep in line with us," Daniel scolded. "If you'd used your taunt where you were, we could have held the group off together."

"I apologise, Friend Daniel. I saw Hero Tula fall, and I fear I acted without thinking," Omrak apologised, flushing with shame. He had worked so hard to train that impulse of out his system, but under the heat of combat in a new environment, he had reverted to his usual tactics.

"It's fine. Just don't do it again," Daniel said and then glanced at Tula.

"I'll stay closer," Tula said with a grimace, still keeping her voice hushed. "Their camouflage was good. But I think I can pick it out in future, knowing what they look like now."

"Good stones!" Asin called back, holding up the stone.

"What... those are B twelves!" Rob exclaimed. His proclamation had the other Adventurers perk up, even Tula taking a moment to glance at the stones. "Those are worth nearly half a silver each."

Asin let out a little chuff of happiness while the rest of the team smiled. Their basking in their newfound wealth was interrupted by Tula a moment later.

"We should move," Tula whispered.

"Lead the way," Daniel said, gesturing for the Ranger to go. Still, he couldn't keep the grin off his face. This Dungeon would likely turn out to be quite profitable.

***

Hours later, the group ascended their fifth hill of the day, grateful for the open ground that meant they were safe from the ambush attacks of the raptors. At the top, Asin and Rob took over watch as Tula squatted and slowly stretched the tension from her body. Being the scout for the group, especially in an area filled with ambush predators, was particularly stressful. Once she had rid herself of the initial stress, Tula immediately unstrung her bow.

"What's that?" Daniel muttered as he pointed to a hill in the distance. He squinted, barely able to ascertain the irregularity on the hill.

Tula looked up from where she had begun inspecting her bow, eyes narrowing for a second as she triggered **Eagle Eye**. A moment later she gasped.

"What?" Rob said.

"It's a fort. Wooden walls, not very large." Tula shrugged and let her Skill fall away. It was impossible to tell more through the mist, even with her Skill.

"And? …" Rob pushed.

"We'll find out later," Daniel cut in, glancing at Tula who had returned to inspecting her bow. "Let's angle towards the keep. I'm guessing that's our objective."

Tula nodded, thankful that Daniel had cut-off Rob but annoyed that the healer had continued to talk afterwards. Could any of them learn to be quiet? Well, other than Asin. Asin was good. In fact, the Catkin would have made an outstanding Ranger with her expanded senses and agility. But as Tula turned to eye the fastidious Catkin who was absently grooming herself while watching for trouble, she discarded the idea once again. No way would the Catkin survive months in the wilderness with no proper showers.

Fingers gently running over the bow, Tula sighed. It was bad for her bow to keep it strung for so long, but with ambush predators constantly harrying them in the Dungeon, she had no choice. Thankfully, the enchantments on her bow helped to reduce the damage that keeping it strung for so long did, but she knew that eventually, she'd have to get a new bow. It was one reason she hated working Dungeons. At least in the wild, a smart, talented and attentive Ranger could avoid most fights.

"How are your arrows doing?" Daniel asked softly as he squatted next to her.

Tula looked up, seeing the too-serious eyes of the healer and could not help but touch her side where a raptor had sneaked a claw in. She pushed aside the memory of pain that insisted on making itself known, instead touching the smooth skin. Healing – such a wonderful gift. Perhaps she should spend more time studying her herbal lore.

"Tula?"

"Good," Tula said, answering Daniel's first question.

"You have enough?" Daniel questioned again and just received a nod. He pursed his lips but just stood instead of saying anything further. As he stood, he called out softly to inform the team. "We're resting for lunch."

In a few minutes, Daniel had a small fire going and a pan over it, with flatbread being softened on the slowly heating pan. On his shield, hastily wiped down, Daniel started slicing up pieces of meat and vegetables to add to the simple meal. Tula's nose wrinkled slightly at his actions but decided to hold off on commenting. This was the Dungeon and the Adventurers had a clearer idea of the dangers at times. Among other things – it wasn't as though they were trying to avoid monsters. And she did like warm food – rarity as it was when she was travelling.

"Gather?" Asin said, pointing to the trail of smoke and then their surroundings. Omrak had taken over Rob's post while the Enchanter, having been informed they'd be staying here for a while, was busy laying down numerous enchanted traps.

"Unlikely," Daniel said, shaking his head. "They're ambush predators. We haven't seen a group larger than five right now, so they're likely to be limited to that amount. And if they did gather, we'll see them long before they can arrive."

"Outside, of course, of the Floor Champion," Omrak rumbled. "It might break your assumptions - as they are wont to do."

"True," Daniel said, rubbing his nose. "But, stronger first floor or not, it's still an Advanced Dungeon's first floor. It's unlikely to be that dangerous."

"Tragic final words," Rob said with a sniff as he ascended the hill. "Try not to leave the hill. If you have to, do recall the markings."

Tula paused in rubbing beeswax on her bow for a moment as her mind flashed over the details that Rob had provided before she left the hill. Purple flowers for ice traps, yellow for spiked traps and green was for poison. Though Rob should not have laid any of the poison traps down since those had a nasty habit of spreading.

"We will," Daniel said without looking up. Soon enough, the healer was serving their lunch which Tula gratefully took. She sat down back at her corner, listening to Rob and Daniel quietly speculate about the new loot drops the raptors had dropped – raptor claws. Thus far, they had collected the claws but as none of them had seen the drops before, they could not gauge their value. That the razor claws dropped once every five or six raptors indicated they were likely to be precious. But likely was not certainly.

"Low Mana flow," Rob said, tapping the claw he had placed in front of him. "Definitely not a channeling enchantment or an empowerment one."

"Channeling? Empowerment?" Daniel parroted dumbly.

"Channeling enchantments allow you to push your Mana through the object, creating a specific effect. Wands, my spikes are good examples," Rob said. "Empowerment enchantments draw Mana from external sources, flow it through the enchantment to create their effects. Asin's bracers are a good example."

"Oh… Then?" Daniel glanced at the razor fang wordlessly.

Rob grunted. "I'm testing. It'd go faster if you let me work…"

Daniel obediently shut his mouth, having learnt his lesson to not bother the easily irritable Mage as he continued to test the object.

After he sat there in silence for a few minutes, Tula looked away, scanning the surroundings for potential problems. As she raised her hand to bite down again a short while later, she felt her teeth clop in empty air, making her flush with embarrassment at having unknowingly finished her food. A quick look around showed that no one had noticed, making Tula sigh in happiness.

"I'd say it's low-level enchantable material. Good for keeping fixed enchantments that benefit the item itself or provide minor boosts to the material around it," Rob said.

"That's it?" Daniel said with a frown.

"A low-level enchantable material is quite rare. Steel is only considered the lowest level material," Rob explained. "While not desirable by Master enchanters, low-level material is the everyday workpiece material for most enchanters."

"Good coin?" Asin asked.

"Decent. Maybe a silver each," Rob said.

The Adventurers grinned wide while Rob scooped the claw back into his pouch. Together, the group stood, dinner finished. Daniel bent low, scooping the waiting dirt into the fire to put it out. Tula stood up, restringing her bow and took the lead without being asked, having already taken bearings for the next hill on the way to the forest. It was time to get back to work, clearing this Floor.

Chapter 6

A clenched fist rose up in the mist and immediately Daniel grew even warier. He stepped sideways, flanking Omrak on the narrow deer trail they travelled on and crouched lower, putting his eyes just above his raised shield as he scanned his side of the trail for trouble. Tula, having warned the group, beckoned them to come again but slowly. Heeding her words, Daniel and team moved forwards slowly while Asin hung back a couple of paces behind Rob to watch over their rear.

As they closed the distance with Tula, Daniel watched for additional hand signals. Soon enough, he realised that Tula was providing none and irritation ate at him. Damn Ranger never felt the need to communicate with the team. After a moment, the more rational part of Daniel pointed out that it could be that Tula actually did not know what had set off her instincts. Intuition was a powerful, if obscure, aid in Dungeons.

As the group reached Tula, she held up her hand sideways once again to ensure none of the party passed her. Daniel, once again, felt a flash of irritation but stayed silent as he tried to spot what it was that had brought their party to a stop. While he was still not as capable as Asin or Tula at spotting the raptors, he had gained some ability over the last few hours.

"What is it?" Rob grumbled as the silence stretched for a time with Tula not moving. Tula shifted at his words before finally, her hand came up, making the signal for trap.

This made Daniel jerk in surprise, and he swung his head back. It took him a moment before he realised what he saw, a simple but well-concealed pitfall trap covered in dirt and fallen leaves laid across the trail. But that moment of inattention cost him, as the waiting raptors exploded from the nearby underbrush, launching their attack.

Instinctively, Daniel swung his shield forward, triggering his **Shield Bash** Skill a moment too soon to catch the raptor full-on. It still struck and sent the monster spiralling backwards, crushing the creature's snout and bloodying its mouth. The raptor let out a low hiss, but Daniel had no time to focus on it further as the rest of its ambush group arrived.

Tula, safe directly behind the pit trap, nocked, drew and loosed an arrow at one of the charging raptors that attempted to jump over the pit trap. Immediately after being loosened, Tula triggered her **Arrow Storm** spell, forming magical copies of the arrow which grouped tightly around the arrow. Together, the momentum from the cluster of arrows caught and halted the monster's jump in mid-air, sending it falling into the middle of the pit trap. The carefully placed thin branches, loose dirt and leaves gave way beneath the monster's weight, sending it falling to be finished off by the spikes in the trap.

On the other side of Daniel, Omrak's great sword kept the pair of raptors that attempted to close in on him back. His initial swing had barely managed to catch one of the monsters, leaving a dripping, bloody wound. At the back, Asin and Rob dealt with the last raptor, it's body already riddled with wounds as the Enchanter's spikes and the Catkin's throwing knives left it injured.

Daniel quickly took in the group, noting that their most vulnerable members were safe and took a step forwards, breaking the line to chase down the raptor. Already, their training from the past week had shown its usefulness. But, as Angie said, there were times to be bold too. Pushing forwards, Daniel focused on finding the perfect time to swing his hammer.

The raptor lunged forwards and then stopped abruptly, swinging its tail around in an attempt to sweep Daniel off his feet. Having been caught before by the sudden change in tactics, Daniel was ready this time and jumped forwards, taking his feet off the ground and slamming his hammer down on the crown of the raptor's head, crushing its skull.

As the raptor flopped bonelessly to the ground, Daniel turned around to view his team and realised the error of focusing too much on his own fight. He had even ignored the shouts of his team as another, larger raptor attacked the back line. Asin lay on the ground near the base of a tree off the trail, shoulder bleeding from where the raptor had bitten her. Now, the larger monster menaced both Tula and Rob who were both bleeding from claw wounds, their paltry melee defenses barely able to keep the monster away.

Quadra Raptor Alpha (Level 12)
Health: 157/180

"Daniel!" Tula shouted again as she ducked another swipe, bringing the large hunting knife she used for melee defense up to threaten the Alpha's eyes. It jerked back, moving away from the threatening knife and swung its head towards Rob whose fingers twisted, shifting the spikes to harass the Alpha and the other injured raptor. In his other hand, a slowly forming **Magic Arrow** began to grow.

Daniel had no time to curse himself as he cast **Minor Healing II** on Asin while he rushed forwards behind his shield. His clumsy, inattentive attack was easily avoided by the Alpha raptor who lashed out with a claw as Daniel closed in, scoring his upper weapon arm. Luckily, his armor caught the majority of the blow. Still, he achieved his objective of pushing the Alpha raptor back.

As he recovered, a kick by the other raptor buckled his foot, leaving long gashes along his leg between the gaps in his armor. On his feet, Daniel groaned but continued to swing his hammer to keep the monsters back. When Rob finally released the empowered **Magic Arrow** against the injured raptor, Daniel took the moment to cast a **Healer's**

Mark on the still-recovering Catkin. The **Magic Arrow** empowered with **Ice** magic crashed into the raptor, freezing its body and slowing its movements.

Armed with a second dagger, Tula moved to flank Daniel, focusing her attention on the injured raptor, cutting and stabbing to disarm the monster. Rob turned as well, unleashing a less powerful **Magic Arrow** to aid the Ranger, leaving Daniel to focus on the Alpha.

Roaring, the Alpha ducked forwards, smashing into Daniel. Daniel staggered backwards, the Skill of the Alpha monster pushing the Adventurer back. With a jump, the creature landed on Daniel's arm, pulling his shield arm down with its claws as it reared forwards to bite. Instead, it was met with a **Double Strike** on its snout, **Find Weakness** intuitively informing Daniel that the tip of its nose was actually extremely weak. Again and again, the hammer smashed into the soft cartilage, crippling the monster and forcing its spasming arms to release his shield arm.

Injured, the Alpha attempted to back off, keening pitifully. Immediately, the remaining raptors attempted to run. Only one managed to get away, the other pair were too injured to escape the wrath of the Adventurers. As the Alpha entered the trees, a cloaked figure tackled it to the ground, dagger threading through its flesh like a sewing needle as Asin exacted her revenge.

"Owww!" Asin complained as she stood up, her impulsive attacks having re-opened the wound on her shoulder. She kicked the monster again and then crouched low, listening to the forest as she waited for the creature to disperse.

"Damn it, healer, your job is to HEAL," Rob snarled, cradling his own injured hand as adrenaline left his body. Blood slowly dripped from the wound, making Daniel wince as he walked over to cast a spell on the Enchanter.

"Sorry," Daniel said with a grimace. He could have explained, but Rob was right. His job, with so many others here, was to stay aware. To heal, rather than to fight. It was the reason he wore so much armor – so that he could take a few moments even in the middle of a fight to check on his friends. It just wasn't easy. "Tula?"

"Healer's Mark," Tula replied, nodding firmly. Daniel eyed the Ranger, spotting some minor cuts but nothing major. Then again, the way she held herself indicated that there might be more serious internal injuries. Torn muscles, bruised internals. Internal bleeding was unlikely, Daniel considered, but he thought he should check. As he placed a hand on Tula's arm, he sent his Gift into her body.

His Gift was strange, unique like all Gifts were, but unique even among the unique Gifts. If that made sense. For his Gift was a healing Gift, one that allowed him to fix problems that would stymie even the most powerful of Healers. But it came with a cost like all Gifts did – in this case, his memories. The more he used his Gift, the higher the cost. Since Daniel was just using the Gift to sense the damage within Tula, the cost was minor, a few seconds here and there. But the information he gained was invaluable.

"You realise the Healer's Mark spell only increases your natural regeneration?" Daniel said softly. "It's like Minor Healing which will forcibly fix an issue. As such, issues like deep internal bleeding or broken bones shouldn't be healed with the Healer's Mark spell, not without the requisite blood or bone being fixed first."

Tula nodded dumbly at Daniel's words and then just stared at the Healer. With a sigh, Daniel decided to just cast the Minor Healing spell. Obviously, Tula didn't understand – or didn't care – that her ribs were moderately misaligned in her chest. Not bad enough that it would cause major problems even with Healer's Mark, but it would be a problem in the future. As the spell hit Tula, the Ranger gasped and straightened explosively and then hunched downwards as if she expected additional pain. When it did not come, her eyes widened with surprise.

"You're welcome," Daniel muttered as he realised that Tula was continuing to be silent. Walking over to Omrak, he readied another spell, only to come to a stop with his jaw hanging down.

"Friend Daniel?"

"You're not injured!" Daniel said.

"I am not."

"But… but…" Daniel sputtered before he came to a stop, realising how insulting his reaction probably was. Thankfully, the good-natured giant did not seem to mind, continuing to nod happily. As the team finished healing and collecting the various loot drops, they gathered again before the pit trap.

"This was not made by the raptors," Omrak said.

"Obviously," Rob replied sarcastically. "The question is, who?"

"Asin?" Daniel asked the Catkin. Asin bent low, sniffing at the trap and eyeing the edges, slowly moving around the edges as she searched for clues. Tula followed as well, eyeing the trap while Daniel and Omrak took to keeping an eye out for new trouble.

"This trap is a Dungeon replication of an existing trap," Tula said softly. "The original was made and absorbed and the Dungeon has then replicated it to this floor."

"There are other monsters on this floor?" Daniel said with a frown.

"Or on the other floors. A borrow from the theme," Rob said. "It is not unheard of."

"Fort," Asin hissed and pointed in the direction they had been travelling. After a moment, Daniel found himself nodding. Of course, the fort had to be staffed by someone, someone who had a tendency to make big, spiked traps. Well…

"Go?" Tula said, pointing down the road as Daniel contemplated. With a shake of his head, Daniel pushed the thoughts aside. In the end, it didn't matter what kind of monsters there were. Their job was to clear as many of them as possible, get the Floor chest and Mana stones and get down to the third floor to deal with the section champion.

Everything else was just details.

"Go."

***

Hours later, the group finally found themselves on top of the nearest clear hill to the fort, their presence hidden behind a convenient set of boulders. The fort itself was much clearer now, a small wooden building which dominated the hills around it. Through the afternoon, the party had fought numerous ambush parties of raptors, the Alpha raptors now a regular addition. With the addition of the Alpha raptors, the monster numbers had also increased, with the group facing up to nine raptors at a time. During those hectic periods, the team would pull in close and face the monsters in a solid line with even Rob and his enchanted spheres being brought to bear. Luckily, each of the Adventurers was Skilled and strong, and through the use of their Skills and tactics, they managed to deal with the monsters without incurring any serious injuries.

In addition to the increase in raptors, the party also noticed the slow increase in the number of traps as they neared the fort. Pitfall traps were common, but other nasty additions were also added. Spike traps made from bent branches, suspended beams of pointed stakes tripped by tripwires, simple noose traps and even simple holes dug into the ground with a single spike in it were laid out all around the Fort. It was at this time that Daniel found Tula's greater experience in the wilderness intensely helpful as the Ranger found, without fail, every single trap they had thus far encountered. It was an astounding success rate, though it did not stop Omrak from accidentally setting off a swinging spike trap by brushing against it too hard.

"Secure fort," the aforementioned Northerner said, eyeing the wooden structure before them and rubbing at his chest where a newly created dimple in his armor rested. The fort was made of a circular set of wooden posts with a single, double-doored wooden gate offering entry. Inside, they could see a smaller wooden structure, and occasionally, it seemed as though creatures patrolled the outer walls. Yet, no matter how hard Daniel squinted, he could not see the figures accurately.

"Who are they?" Daniel muttered.

"Unclear," Tula said, squinting for a time before relaxing her shoulders and eyes.

"Same," Rob said as he lowered a small circular object from his eyes. At Daniel's curious glance he showed him the simple spyglass etched with runes on it. "It seems there is some magical interference."

"I don't like this," Daniel said.

"Fear not, Friend Daniel. Whatever knave trickery the Dungeon may bring, we shall beat it with our force of arms," Omrak said, patting his friend on the shoulder. "For our cause is just."

"But they don't seem to be reacting to our presence either," Daniel said, tapping his lips. "Do you think they are restricted to their fort?"

"It is possible. Such circumstances are not unknown among Dungeon floors. It is possible that they might not be able to ascertain our presence either, like we theirs," Rob said.

"Camp?" Asin asked, butting in and pointing deeper into the boulder ring. This hill seemed to be the perfect camping spot with both a defensible position and a good environment to block off the wind. As Daniel looked up to gauge the time, he realised once again that this Dungeon had no moon or starts to tell the time against. Rather than do that, he eyed his team and their condition.

"Camp. No fire," Daniel finally commanded, having gauged that the group was tired. He was too, with his Mana nearly drained. While they had managed to traverse the first floor with minimal on-going injuries, the truth was that he had to use his spells numerous times to ensure the battle readiness of them all. Better to rest tonight and tackle the challenge of the fort tomorrow.

Chapter 7

After an early start, it took them only a few hours to arrive at the bottom of the hill that led up to the fort. Together, the team looked at one another and then focused on Daniel, awaiting his orders.

"Let's try to go up quietly," Daniel said softly, looking in particular at Tula. The Ranger nodded, eyeing the slope of the hill and the underbrush for a moment through the mist before guiding them sideways for a bit before she began the ascent.

The Ranger travelled upwards slowly, stopping occasionally to gauge her surroundings. As they climbed, the mist that surrounded the group slowly parted, revealing more and more of the hill, allowing Tula to speed up her pathfinding. It was when the mist fully dissipated that Tula stopped, unnerved by a new phenomenon. When the team finally gathered next to Tula, they all found themselves staring at the slight shimmer in the air ahead of them.

"What is that?" Daniel finally voiced the question in all their minds.

"That -" Rob said slowly as he lowered his enchanted spyglass, "- is a portal. Probably to the next floor."

"Already?" Omrak said, surprised.

"That's a portal?" Daniel frowned. "It's not bright and swirly like the others."

"That is because those other portals are poorly made. On purpose," Rob said. When the other Adventurers looked at the Enchanter for an explanation, he smirked and straightened further. "You see, the initial Dungeons created by Panqua all hosted portals such as these. They still do. But it seemed that accidentally stepping through a portal into another floor brought less than stellar results. As such, all portals since then have been *degraded* to give sufficient allowance."

"Portal good," Asin said as she pointed forwards. Then pointed upwards. "Portal bad."

"Yes," Rob said bitingly as Asin succinctly explained his point. "It is, of course, quite interesting why Panqua would create such a portal here. I wonder if he wished to experiment at keeping the theme of the location constant. After all, the fort is sufficient warning."

"Maybe," Daniel said with a shrug. "Tula?"

The Ranger hesitated at Daniel's question as she eyed the portal again. Even with Rob's assurance that it was unlikely to be a trap and just something that was meant to be there, the Ranger's natural caution made her hesitate.

"It is my honour to enter such areas first," Omrak said as he moved to stand up. A hand on his arm stilled him and the giant Northerner stared at Daniel in confusion. "Yes?"

"Tula, can you point out a good route for Omrak? Bring him as close as you can before he can enter it," Daniel said. The Ranger nodded quickly and led Omrak along a meandering path up the hill. The path, like all those she had chosen thus far, kept the pair out of sight of those above as much as possible. Once they reached a spot a bare five feet from the mildly shimmering air that indicated the start of the portal, Tula stopped. Omrak did not, tromping straight in, disappearing from their view.

"Oh…" Daniel said in surprise. Then he cursed himself. Of course, there would be nothing to see. It was a portal after all. Realising his friend was now left on the other side of a potentially hostile portal, Daniel waved the team to get up and move.

In minutes, the group had regrouped on the other side of the portal, none the worse for wear. In fact, the transition itself had been more comfortable than any they had thus far experienced. After a brief survey of the land around, which, surprisingly, looked exactly the same as the land they had seen before, the team continued their ascent.

***

In less than an hour, she led the group to a small dip in the hill, one that provided a good view of the fort without exposing them. It was there that the group received the first surprise of the day.

"Orcs," Tula said softly to the group, her eyes squinting as she activated her **Eagle Eye** Skill.

"That's new," Daniel muttered. Even this morning, they were unable to assess the humanoid figurines on the walls. It seemed that Rob's conjecture that the portal here had been planned to be just another extension to the floor was correct. Daniel frowned, edging upwards to stare at the monsters. At this distance, they were small figures, but detailed enough for Daniel to tell that they were indeed Orcs – tusked, muscular and armed with simple leather armour. Interestingly enough, unlike the green-skinned brethren in the outside world, these Orcs were all black skinned. "Tula, can you tell anything else?"

"Too far to get a status update on their levels," Tula said softly. "But they're armed and armored. Lousy armor, I can see the wear and lack of care from even here. Three… no, four patrolling the walls. The gates are closed too."

"Ba'al's tears," Daniel said, swearing softly. Of course, the gate was closed. And since this was a Dungeon, it was unlikely to open either for things like trade, returning scouts or the retrieval of water. Obviously, the challenge for this floor included determining how to enter the forts.

Still, it puzzled Daniel why the floor was built like this. Why separate the fort via a portal from the first floor? Was the second floor so small that it contained only a single fort? Of course, the fort itself could be spatially distorted within – larger on the inside than the outside – but it made little sense for Panqua to waste even more of his energy to do that. With no answer to his questions, Daniel pushed the thought aside to focus on how they were to gain entry.

"Recommendations?" Daniel asked.

"Night. Climb. Kill. Open," Asin said.

"There are four guards," objected Daniel. "And it's such a small fort, it'd be easy for others to spot you when you're opening the gate."

"We could break down the doors," Omrak said. "They do not look too sturdy. It would be a simple matter to acquire a modified battering ram."

Silence greeted Omrak's proposal. After a moment, Omrak grinned at them and the group exhaled with relief.

"You were joking," Daniel said with relief.

"I was," Omrak said. "It is not a plan even my second brother would make."

"Jokes aside, we still need to get in. Rob, could you destroy the gate?" Daniel asked with some hope. He was a mage after all. They wielded the powers of nature.

"I'm an Enchanter specialist, not an Evocation specialist," Rob said grumpily. "Even if I enhanced my **Magic Arrow** to its maximum, it still wouldn't do more than dent the gate."

"Damn," Daniel said. He then looked at Tula who shrugged her shoulders.

"I could take an Orc or two out with my bow, but it would still leave the gate locked," Tula said.

"Ah, that I can help with," Rob interrupted. "A simple application of **Magical Hand** will allow me to engage the bar and move it aside."

"Aren't those things heavy?" Daniel said.

"Yes. But well within the limitations of my spell," Rob answered with a sniff. "If needed, I can open the gate - providing I am close enough to cast my spell."

"Stealth. Mage. Not good," Asin pointed out. Rob could not help but nod at that, willing to concede that his ability at sneaking – as shown in the last few weeks – was less than spectacular. Dismal even.

"Could Tula and Asin deal with the guards? Allowing the rest of us the opportunity to sneak closer," Omrak said, pointing at the fort. "We then open the gates and slay all those within."

"Which we don't know is how many," Daniel pointed out with a grimace. "There could be quite a few."

"And I would prefer not to charge into a fully manned fort," Rob added. After that, the team fell silent as they pondered what to do, Tula continuing to watch the still fort. A few minutes later, Daniel looked up and excitedly repeated his idea.

***

In truth, the plan was simplistic. If they did not know how many were within, they should find out. And the easiest way to do so was to bait the Orcs out. With that in mind, the team had taken a short journey down from the hill to set up a trap before sending Tula and Asin back up the hill. Tula would take the shot or shots, killing as many of the sentries as possible before the Orcs were alerted. Eventually, they conjectured, the Orcs would send someone after the lone Ranger. Asin would stay hidden, there as backup and to flank the monsters when they launched their attack.

Waiting at the bottom of the hill, lurking behind a convenient tree, Daniel could only hope that his plan worked. It was predicated upon the fact that the Orcs would react to some extent like their non-Dungeon counterparts – that is, with thinking grace and flexibility. No sentient race would allow an archer, especially one as skilled as Tula to continue to provoke them without retaliation. The Orcs could, perhaps, send archers or crossbowmen of their own against her – but a lone archer of her Skill would easily outmatch and depart if they chose that route. No. Mounted cavalry or light infantry would be the best option.

Soon enough, Daniel heard the sound of growing clamour from above. Indistinct shouts laced with anger and fury bore down upon them, the loud – very loud – creaking of the gates as they swung open and then the quick pitter-patter of feet running down the hill as Tula came. Occasionally, Tula would stop and the twang of a bow followed by muted shouts would appear. A short while later, the Ranger appeared at the top of the path, jogging lightly with a smile on her face. She jumped lightly over the line of flowers, then weaved past the other traps before skidding to a stop just beside a boulder, crouching low and nocking another arrow.

Following the Ranger were a half-dozen Orcs clad in chainmail tunics, padded pauldrons and a gorget. A banded metal and leather skirt helped protect their lower body while the majority of the Orcs carried spears. All but a single mace-and-shield wielding leader who bled freely from an arrow that jutted from his stomach.

Orc Sargent (Level 14)
Health: 184/210

Orc Spearmen (Level 11)
Health: 140/140

The moment the Orcs rounded the path and began to shake out into formation, Tula loosed her first arrow. This time, rather than targeting the Sargent who hung towards the back of the crowd, she sent an arrow into the calf of one of the spear-wielding Orcs, forcing it to kneel as the arrow lamed it. The Orc Sargent roared, and the group finished setting up quickly and began a fast march towards Tula even as she nocked another arrow. This time, when she launched the attack, an Orc in the center glowed with a green light and the arrow deflected into the air as its Skill functioned.

Without breaking stride, Tula immediately drew and nocked another arrow as the group rushed her. As she drew and sighted the bow, she hesitated on loosing just long enough for the fast-approaching Orcs to hit the first line of traps. The lead Orc kicked the strung wire, triggering the enchantment laid beneath their feet which exploded from the ground in spikes of ice. Reacting instinctively, the Orcs jumped and twisted, disrupting their formation in an attempt to escape the attack.

It was then that Tula loosed her arrow, drawing and nocking another even as Daniel and Omrak stood up and attacked with their own ranged weapons. Daniel's long-unused crossbow twanged, its deadly bolt winging through the air to take an Orc in the stomach where the bolt punched through the chainmail links with ease. Omrak's throwing axe was less successful as it was deflected by the haft of a spear to land harmlessly on the ground. Immediately, Omrak reached for his second throwing axe while Daniel dropped his crossbow and exited around the boulder to take station in front of Tula.

"Invaders!" One of the less startled and injured Orcs shouted as he struggled to his feet, the spear levelled. In seconds, the remainder of the surviving Orcs lined up. There was a total of three Orc Spearmen in line now, one of which favored a lamed leg where an ice spike had punched through its reinforced boots. A second Orc Spearman lay on the ground, doubly lamed from arrow and ice spike. Behind them, the Orc Sargent looked on grimly at his diminished troop.

"Traps," the Orc Sargent hawked and spat. As if the curse was a command, another Orc Spearman strode a single step forward over the triggered ice spike trap and slammed its spear into the ground, angled towards Tula. It then jerked backwards as Tula's arrow smashed into its shoulder, embedding itself. Injured or not, the Orc's Skill sent a ripple through the ground and triggered the remainder of Rob's enchantments, releasing their stored energies uselessly.

"What a waste!" Rob snarled as his set traps triggered with little result.

Daniel almost cursed him out for revealing his presence, but decided against it, keeping his focus on the now fast-approaching Orcs. Even Tula had decided against staying on the front lines, having slung her bow over one shoulder and proceeded to scramble up a nearby boulder for a better vantage point for the ensuing melee battle. Omrak strode forward, all of his throwing axes expanded with little to show for it, and joined Daniel on the front-lines.

"Charge on my command," Daniel bit out. Omrak offered a slight nod in reply as he readied his greatsword.

"Now!"

Together, the pair charged the group of four Orcs. Another arrow whizzed by the pair, splitting in mid-air as it approached the group and forming an **Arrow Storm**. Without shields, the Orc Spearmen could only weather the attack and charge forwards. Even the disciplined monsters could not help but slow slightly, disrupting their formation as the empowered **Piercing arrows** in the **Arrow Storm** struck, injuring another pair. Then the charging parties met.

Daniel ducked at the last moment while bringing his shield upwards, deflecting the spear over his head. The rush of air as it skimmed above him set Daniel's heart hammering in his chest. Staying focused, the stocky Adventurer put his shoulder into the shield as he rushed the Orc Spearman, over-running the monster and leaving a wildly swung hammer strike on the Orcs shoulder as he passed. Spinning on his heel, Daniel barely managed to deflect the mace strike from the Orc Sargent before he set himself behind his shield, ready to buy time for his friends to finish off the Orcs.

Not that the Orc Sargent was going to give him a significant amount of time to watch the rest of his party as it launched attack after attack against Daniel. A sudden flicker in the Orc Sargent's body was the only warning that Daniel received before the Orc Sargent suddenly sped up, the first strike sending his shield out of place. The second and third smashed into Daniel's chest, the last slightly deflected as he felt his breastplate warp and his breath explode from his chest.

Before the Sargent could take further advantage of Daniel, a throwing knife flashed forwards and struck his shoulder, punching through its armor under the effects of Asin's Skill. In the meantime, Daniel automatically reached inwards with his Gift to heal the damage done to him. The Catkin loped forwards, throwing knives spinning out to harass the other Orc Spearmen who fought Omrak. Together with the Enchanter and the Ranger, the Northerner had managed to lay low one of his opponents already and was fending off the attacks of the other pair.

Seeing that his friends had the other Orcs managed, Daniel focused on the Orc Sargent. His Find Weakness Skill blared at him, but amusingly, offered little additional knowledge that he did not know – temple, armpit, groin, knee – all the areas where the monster had less armor. Instead, Daniel waited until the Orc Sargent was forced to block a throwing knife to his face before he acted. With the monster's shield in its face, it could do nothing when Daniel triggered **Shield Bash** to slam the offending piece of defensive equipment into the Orc's snout. As it staggered backwards, Daniel swung his hammer upwards at an angle with full strength, impacting the monster's kidney and shattering its armor as he triggered **Perrin's Blow**. The powerful attack Skill lifted the monster off its feet before it crashed to the ground, stunned. With a quick step, Daniel placed his weight on the monster's mace and began to strike at the prone monster which struggled to hide behind its shield.

A few blows later, including one that struck the crown of the Orc Sargent's head, Daniel finally killed his opponent. Of course, he could have finished it a little earlier, but he had taken the time to check on his friends as a good healer was supposed to. That his friends had done fine - their combined attacks having firstly injured then killed the Orcs - had allowed the Adventurer to focus on his own attacks.

Daniel gulped some air down, the helmet once again stifling his breathing. He frowned up the pathway and then glanced at Tula who had a better viewpoint. She shook her head in the negative. It was then that the healer began to relax and review his friends. After a moment, he smiled as he realised no one was injured. Well, other than him.

"That was a glorious battle!" Omrak said, grinning widely. "Now what?"

"Now…" Daniel paused, considering. "We do it again. Rob?"

"I'll recharge my enchantments. Not that it mattered," Rob grumbled as he walked towards his traps. Asin happily ran around picking up the Mana stones from the dispersed monster bodies, pocketing them after a brief inspection. By this time, the better than normal drops had become routine.

"Skirt?" Asin said as she trotted back, holding one of the armored skirts up for the group. After a moment, Daniel realised that the delay in Asin joining the battle had been due to her backstabbing and killing the injured Orcs. Nasty, but effective.

"Cursed?" Daniel shot back. Asin shrugged and walked to Rob to interrogate the Enchanter. A minute later, the Catkin was back, grinning widely.

"No. Not enchanted," Asin said and offered it again to Daniel.

"Not me. Omrak?" Daniel said. The skirt would do little to add to his defense and just slow him down with the additional weight.

"Mmm…" Omrak took it from Asin, eyeing the entire ensemble before he shrugged and put it on. He posed for a bit, tapping and banging on the skirt and adjusting his belt to ensure it kept his pouches within easy reach. "Thank you."

Asin nodded back with a grin, crouching back down as she waited for Rob to be done.

"Anything?" Daniel called up to Tula.

"Nothing. They seem to just be waiting," Tula said.

"Okay then. We'll take the gift," Daniel said. "Once Rob is done, we'll hit them again and see if we can draw more out."

Chapter 8

"Nothing?" Daniel grumbled when Tula came back. It seemed that the Orcs had decided not to be baited a second time, even when Tula had shot at their men. They, in turn, had chosen to pull their people off the walls. Without a target, Tula had eventually decided to make her way back to the team to report in, leaving Asin to watch the fort for changes.

Tula nodded, and Daniel sighed. He had hoped the Orcs would have been 'kind' enough to donate a few more bodies to the cause, but a single squad seemed to be the extent of what they could expect. Decision made, Daniel waved the group up the hill where they crouched at the same location they had been at earlier in the day. As they eyed the seemingly deserted fort, Daniel could not help but frown at the slowly darkening 'sky'.

"We need to finish this before night comes," Daniel declared. "We'll use Rob's plan."

"It's not…" Rob began to protest but the rest of the group had already started moving out. "My plan." Rob finished to empty air before he sighed and followed after the group.

With Tula watching over her, Asin quickly scaled the fort's wall silently while the team gathered at the bottom of the wall, hiding near the gates. Rob had already begun channeling his **Magic Hand** spell to pull the bar of the gate off. When Asin was just below the edge of the wall Daniel nodded to Rob who released his spell.

A giant, floating hand appeared, glowing with an ethereal power. With a grunt, Rob shoved the hand into the gate itself, the semi-solid hand passing through the wooden gate with resistance. Surprised shouts erupted from within the fort at the intrusion. An Orc decided to push its head above the fort's walls, only to fall backwards with an arrow sticking out of its eye. Taking the Orcs sudden presence as the sign to move, Asin clambered the rest of the way up the wall to provide an additional distraction as Rob struggled to open the gates.

Muted shouts and screams continued to filter through the wooden walls before a loud boom of the gate's bar falling alerted the party of Rob's success. As the Enchanter jerked his hands back and yanked the gate open, Omrak and Daniel scurried out from their hiding spot, ranged weapons ready.

What greeted them as the doors swung wide open were a line of Orcs and raptors. Except, these raptors were larger than the four-foot-tall creatures they had initially met with bigger heads but weirdly proportioned tiny arms. They were so large in fact that a trio of Orcs sat on the raptors and, when the doors opened, they kicked the raptors to charge the pair. Behind the trio of charging Orcs, a quartet of Orc Spearmen charged after, goaded on by another Orc Sargent.

Lomak Raptor (Level 14)
Health: 190/190

Orc Raptor Rider (Level 13)
Health: 160/160

"Ba'al's Curse!" Daniel shouted as he threw himself out of the way. Omrak, on the other hand, chose to stand his ground, moving only at the last moment to cut with his great sword at the Lomak Raptor's foot as the monster charged past. His movement was executed beautifully, perfectly timed and it sent the raptor sprawling, its rider forced to throw himself into a roll to avoid being crushed. But this action left Omrak vulnerable to the Orc Spearmen that charged after, one of whom managed to sink a spear into the upper left of the Northerner's chest.

Bleeding and stuck, the Northerner was pushed back by his attacker as the other spearmen began to crowd the giant and stab at him with their spears. Each strike that drew blood increased the red glow around Omrak. With a snarl, Omrak grabbed the spear tip with his left hand, using his greater strength to pull it out of his shoulder as he set his feet. As the Orc Spearman attempted to wrest control of his spear back, Omrak chopped downwards, parting the Orc Spearman's hand at the cost of another spear strike burying itself in his torso. As Omrak groaned and battered another spear away, a white wave of power washed over him, visibly healing some of his wounds. Another moment later, a pulse of healing energy filled him.

Spells cast to keep his friend alive a little longer, Daniel crouched again behind his shield as the remaining pair of Orc Raptor Riders came by for another pass, hammering his shield and attempting to bowl over the stocky Adventurer. Luckily for Daniel, the raptors themselves were less interested in forcibly running over the Adventurer, content to run past him and claw at his armored body. Even protected by shield and plate armor, Daniel received a few surface cuts and significant bruises as the enemies charged pass. He knew that he would not last another such charge.

Luckily, he did not need to do so as Tula and Rob focused their efforts on one of the raptor riders as he rode away, launching arrows and spikes at him. Their attacks drew the Orc away from Daniel as he then proceeded to charge Rob who stood before him, weaving an empowered Ice Magic Arrow. The Orc had only a brief moment to realise that the Enchanter was smirking slightly before the Lomak Raptor he was riding hit the prepared Spike Trap, laming the monster and throwing him from the beast to land beside Rob. As the Orc Rider struggled to its feet, he received the Magic Arrow to his face, the empowered Ice enchantment spreading to cover his nose and throat, suffocating the monster.

As Daniel stood up and watched the other Lomak raptor turn around to charge him, he briefly eyed the fight around him. Asin had dropped down from behind into the now-abandoned fort but was engaged in a duel with the Orc Sargent. The fast Catkin evaded the monster's attacks with ease, content to 'kite' the monster and occasionally send a throwing knife into the tense melee around Omrak.

It was Omrak – who now fought both the remaining Spearmen and the unraptored Rider – whose position was most perilous. Against the spear wielders, the giant's greater reach was negated, leaving him constantly backing off to stop from being surrounded. Even then, blood streamed from the Adventurer, muscle and flesh hanging from wounds torn open. The dark red glow from his rage ability surrounded Omrak, a testament to the amount of damage already done.

"Omrak!" Daniel's eyes widened, fear showing as a spear plunged into the Northerner's foot, pinning him. Before he could cast another spell, the Raptor Rider was back, the momentary distraction sufficient to let the rider slam his sabre into Daniel's helmet, making it ring.

"I. Shall. Not. FALL!" Omrak roared as he caught one spear and blocked another before he triggered his Skill, **the Lightning's Call**. The red glow around Omrak disappeared into his body, replaced by bolts of lightning. Caught by surprise, the Spearmen and Rider were unable to dodge the fast-moving, shocking attack which shocked and stunned them. Omrak sagged to the ground after the attack, discarding the stolen spear to blindly reach for a Healing potion.

"Stupid!" Asin growled as she dashed out the gates, closely followed by the Orc Sargent.

Strong as the Sargent might be, he was unable to keep up with the swift-footed Catkin who bounded over to a recovering Orc Rider and **backstabbed** him, plunging her knife in the gap between the monster's neck and torso armor. The blade easily slid all the way in, the critical strike tearing through muscle, bone and arteries with similar ease. With a light hop, the Catkin jumped into the air and spun, her throwing knife flashing as a **Fan of Knives** blossomed to attack the following Sargent. Impressive as her attack was, Asin landed with a heavier thump than normal, her breathing ragged as her stamina drained through her liberal use of Skills.

"Focus on healing," Tula said as she dashed over to haul Daniel to his woozy feet. Immediately afterwards, the Ranger pulled an arrow from her quiver, nocking it and eyeing the rampaging Raptor and Rider. Daniel absently noted how blood dripped from her bow hand to the ground as he forced his Gift to heal his aching head. Daniel was once again thankful that his understanding of his own body was extensive enough that he could use his Gift on himself during combat – a feat that was nearly impossible and highly dangerous on others.

As his head cleared, Daniel saw Rob running directly away from his former opponent towards Omrak, a small ball in his hand. Eyes wide, Daniel began casting another **Minor Healing** spell on Omrak as the now lobbed ball of poison exploded at the giant's feet. Within seconds, the purplish cloud of poison had diffused through the group, poisoning the now-recovered Spearmen and the Northerner alike.

"Don't poison our people!" Daniel growled softly. Still, as Rob came to a stop and sent his pair of spikes to aid Omrak, he knew that the Enchanter had chosen correctly. In fact, he had probably done more right than Daniel had. Another spell washed over Omrak, taking the Northerner from dangerously close to death to only within waving distance.

"Rider," Tula warned. Daniel glanced back and realised that Tula had loosed her arrow, sending a **Piercing Strike** into the raptor's chest, making it veer away from them. Rather than follow his steed, the Raptor Rider had jumped off and was running towards the pair.

"Together," Daniel said to Tula even as Asin and Rob moved to support Omrak as he limped out of the fast-dispersing poison cloud. Hefting his hammer, Daniel made himself focus as he began to trade blows with the Rider. After a few moments of fighting, his **Find Weakness** gift informed him of a surprising weakness. As the Orc swung again, Daniel triggered his **Shield Bash**, counter-attacking the sabre swing in mid-strike. The unexpected movement and a weakness in the Orc's grip made the sabre spin away into the air, a motion that left the Rider surprised. Long enough for Tula to step out from behind Daniel and put an arrow into its throat.

Even as the pair rejoiced, the initially lamed raptor and the unridden raptor finally made their way towards Daniel and Tula, attacking the pair. Daniel snarled, realising that this fight had yet to be finished.

***

"I'm sorry," Daniel said softly to Omrak, and then again loudly to his friends. Hand on the giant's body, he alternately cast his **Minor Healing** spell on the Northerner and used his Gift to guide Omrak's body to speed up its healing. Even as he did so, Daniel felt a portion of his memories – a cuddle with his grandfather, a lesson on spelling, a fight in the Dungeon – slip away. Yet, Daniel could not help but feel it was a worthy trade, insufficient penance.

"For what?" Tula asked, frowning as she inspected her retrieved arrows.

"I broke the line," Daniel said. "If I had stayed with Omrak, he wouldn't have been injured as much."

"Or you would have both been ridden over," Rob said. "While the raptors were reluctant to do so, if you had barred their way entirely, it is likely they would have ridden you over. And while your armor is good, it is not that good."

Daniel grunted, but then shook his head. "I should have at least reconnected with Omrak immediately after instead of standing around, fighting the raptors and their riders."

"Tried. Too many," Asin said as she rubbed her leg. Daniel made a note to check on her soon after, though he was pretty certain it was just a strained muscle. One that his **Healer's Mark** would fix soon. In fact, Daniel had to admit, while everyone had walked away with injuries, other than Omrak, none were life-threatening. Well, except the aneurysm that he had fixed on himself. But they didn't need to know that.

"Of greater concern is the sheer number of enemies we faced," Rob said and then eyed the still open gates. "If anything, our failure this time was due to a lack of scouting."

"Yes," Tula said then grimaced. "I should have insisted."

"Why didn't you?" Daniel said, curiously. Not that he was going to blame their erstwhile scout for not insisting on doing her job properly.

Tula fell silent for so long that Daniel thought she was not about to answer. When she did, her voice was softer than ever. "I wanted us to clear the floor first."

"Competitive," Asin said.

Tula looked up, about to protest and then saw the wide grin on Asin's face. The Ranger flushed slightly before she finally nodded.

"Well, we won't make that same mistake again," Daniel said as he finished with Omrak. "Alright, who's next?"

***

The fort itself was disappointing to the Adventurers, sitting empty and barren when explored. Made of wood and clay, the ground floor of the fort consisted of a large gathering hall that obviously acted as the dining hall as well for the building. Leading from the main hall were rooms for the – now barren – armory and kitchen. Surprisingly, the kitchen itself yielded a bounty of meat, fresh vegetables and a yellowish-orange potato that the Adventurers took to refill their provisions. Upstairs, the rooms consisted of a number of simple sleeping quarters. In a corner of the largest room, next to the bed, a chest lay.

"What's in it?" Rob asked impatiently.

"Shhh…" Asin hissed as she gently ran fingers along the chest. She'd already checked with first a feather then a pick, but now, she was reviewing it with her fingers.

"Patience," Daniel reiterated to Rob. "Unless you are volunteering to open it."

"That is the Catkin's job," Rob said with a sniff. "Though I have considered learning an Open Lock spell."

"Why don't you?" Omrak asked.

"Learning new spells is a significant undertaking. Both in terms of the funds required as well as the time taken. I could as easily upgrade my knowledge of enchantments during the same period rather than delving into such mundane topics."

"Then why mention it?" Daniel asked.

"Because it always takes so long!" Rob groused. The other Adventurers all rolled their eyes, even Tula who stood outside the room watching the corridor. Just in case.

"Safe," Asin finally declared before she extracted her lock picks. She bent down low, eyeing the keyhole again before extracting a pair of lock picks. In a few minutes – and after Daniel sent Rob and Omrak to 'continue' the search – she opened the chest.

"Don't," Daniel said when Asin moved to open the chest. "Let's get everyone here."

Asin just nodded, sitting back on her haunches as Daniel called for the others. When everyone finally gathered, Asin pushed the chest open without fanfare. Eyes wide, the Adventurers exchanged looks before Rob broke the disappointed silence.

"EMPTY!" the Enchanter waved his hands around. "It's *empty*!"

"We can see that," Daniel said and shot a look to Asin. The Catkin nodded and started prodding around the inside of the chest.

"Ah! A secret compartment. Of course," Rob said, subsiding. But when the Catkin sat back after a time and shook her head, he growled. "You must have missed something. There's no reason for there to be an empty chest!"

"Empty."

"You're wrong. Break it open!" Rob said, reaching for his own knife. When Asin glanced at Daniel, he shrugged and waved her aside. The Catkin sniffed, hopping backwards onto a bed without looking while Rob advanced and stabbed the red lining, tearing the chest apart. Minutes later, the Enchanter sat back, disappointed.

"This makes no sense," Rob complained. "All that, for nothing? Why put a chest here if there's no reward? Is Panqua teasing us?"

"Perhaps," Omrak said. "Or perhaps there is no Mana Stone for there is no Champion."

"Champion..." Tula said the words softly then eyed the single bed before her eyes widened. "The Floor Champion. Maybe he didn't spawn yet!"

"Or he spawned and was killed by the other team," Daniel said with a shrug. "It could be that the respawn rate of normal monsters is faster than for the Champion."

"Erlis' tears," Rob cursed and then stood up, sheathing his knife. "Fine. Let's go. Where're the stairs to the next floor."

Silence resounded through the group as they realised that none of them had spotted anything like that. The fort did not even have a basement, which meant the only staircase around lead upwards. After the group went through the fort one last time in search of hidden rooms or staircases – which, when you considered the fort literally had only two sets of internal walls, was incredibly unlikely – the group gave up. By this time, they were all moving around in the relative darkness of the night.

"Do we stay here and risk a respawn directly on us or go outside?" Daniel asked his team.

"Respawns in locations which consist of Adventurers are low probability events," Rob said.

"Huh?" Omrak looked at Rob, confused.

"No respawns likely," Daniel translated for Omrak.

"Stay," Asin said and pointed upwards. "Bed."

"We should still have a watch. And close the gates," Tula said.

"Okay. Rob, close the gates. Asin, you have dinner. Omrak, you have last shift," Daniel began before listing the rest of the shifts for watch. As Tula volunteered for the first shift, Daniel quietly gave himself the middle shift of the night. While his Gift could not remove his need for sleep entirely, he could reduce the effects on him.

And perhaps tomorrow, in the light of day, they could work out where the entrance for the third floor was.

Chapter 9

"That's new," Daniel said as he squinted into the distance.

A quiet evening had led to the group waking up and tackling the mystery of the missing way down with vigor in the morning. A thorough check of the fort had provided no additional clues and so the team had expanded their test to check over the entirety of the hill. Hours later, the group had to reluctantly accept that the way down was not on that particular hill. Together, they had exited through the nearly perfectly transparent portal. As they looked around in search of their next objective, Daniel had spotted the anomaly.

"Definitely not there before," Tula said.

Daniel could only concur with the Ranger as he eyed the minimap his **Mapping** II Skill had created. If the fort which now existed on that hill had been present before they had entered the second floor, it would have shown up on his map.

"Behind," Asin hissed.

Startled by her tone, the group spun around only to be greeted by another perplexing mystery. The fort which they had just exited had now disappeared without a trace, leaving an empty hill behind.

"Ba'al!" Omrak cursed as he unsheathed his sword. After a time, when no threat emerged from the mist or from behind them, the big Northerner sheathed his sword sheepishly.

"Rob?" Tula queried their resident know-it-all.

"This…" Rob paused, falling silent and stroking his chin. After a time, he looked up with a knowing smirk. "Of course. It's a new set-up. Panqua must be testing a new format for the Dungeons."

"But what does it mean?" Daniel hissed in frustration. "Are we going to have to travel to that fort and fight it again? Why?"

"If I'm allowed to speculate, I would assume that is so. It seems that the second floor, instead of being a single location is instead made of linked forts. I would assume that we must destroy or clear a sufficient number of such buildings before we are able to locate the way down."

"Maybe not down," Asin added.

"Yes. Well pointed out. There might not be a third floor. The next location might just be a different landscape," Rob said.

"Ah. So, we must slay more Orcs to progress," Omrak rumbled, his grin widening. "Good. I feel that I did not account for myself in our last encounter. I look forward to meeting these Orcs again."

With little to gain from staying still, Daniel waved the group onwards to the next hill. As usual, the group would travel from hill to hill in their attempts to reduce the amount of time spent in the mists and subject to the attacks of the raptors.

***

As Daniel rested on the hill before the group was to tackle the next fort, he eyed the notification that had appeared after their last encounter with the raptors.

Level Up!
Adventurer Level 12

You have gained 5 attribute points and 1 skill proficiencies.

"Anyone else level?" Daniel asked, looking around the group.

"Yesterday," Asin said.

"About two hours ago," Omrak said agreeably. Daniel could not help but grimace, knowing that their faster leveling speed had more to do with his constant use of his Gift than any difference in experience.

"Rob? Tula?"

"No," Rob said curtly.

"Soon," Tula added.

"How soon? Will you get a Skill point?" Daniel asked Tula. Stopping and returning to fight monsters to give her her next Level might be worthwhile if Tula could gain another Class Skill.

"No," Tula shook her head. "Level 15 next."

"Oh…" Daniel grimaced at how much of a difference there was. "Rob, Tula. You're on watch. We'll distribute our points then."

After getting confirming nods, Daniel pulled up his character sheet and considered his next steps. First, he had to allocate his attribute points. The first thing he did was add a point to Constitution. He kept getting battered around, especially as he took on more roles in their fights. Better to ensure he had less chance of dying by increasing his Constitution, even if it was by a small amount.

Next up, he added two points to his Intelligence stat. That would see a small increase in the on-going gains for his Mana pool from now on, which was important as he expanded on his role as a healer. In fact, Daniel was almost tempted to sink more points into the ability but he also wanted to increase both his Luck and Willpower. Those, he increased by a point each.

Luck was a necessary component for any Adventurer. Too many things could go wrong when delving, and without Erlis's finger on the scale, it was too easy for an Adventurer to die. While he did not put a large amount into it, Adventurers like Husa Light Feet were a perfect example of what a Luck build could do. Of course, most school children were warned against following his example as it was an extremely weak build in the early periods.

As for Willpower, this was a hedge for future floors. Every Adventurer knew that mental attacks were something that Master Class Adventurers had to deal with in their Dungeons. Even on the deeper floors of an Advanced Dungeon, it was quite possible to meet the occasional mentat. An Adventurer with insufficient Willpower at that point was nothing more than a hindrance to their party.

Once he had applied his points, Daniel checked his character sheet to verify where his skills were at.

Name: Daniel Chai (Advanced Rank Adventurer)

Race: Human (Male)

Class: Level 12 Adventurer (0%)

Sub-classes: Level 7 (Miner) (2.4%)

Life: 327

Stamina: 327

Mana: 242

Attributes

Strength: 29

Agility: 25

Constitution: 32

Intelligence: 26

Willpower: 21

Luck: 17

Skills

Unarmed Combat: Level 8 (52/100)

Clubs (Novice): Level 7 (11/100)

Archery: Level 3 (04/100)

Shield (Novice): Level 6 (98/100)

Dodge (Novice): Level 1 (83/100)

Combat Sense (Novice): Level 4 (69/100)

Perception (Novice): Level 3 (14/100)

Mining: Level 7 (78/100)

Healing (Novice): Level 4 (23/100)

Herb Lore: Level 3 (48/100)

Stealth: Level 2 (39/100)

Cooking: Level 4 (13/100)

Singing: Level 2 (14/100)

Tactics: Level 3 (21/100)

Skill Proficiencies

Double Strike

Shield Bash

Perin's Blow

Find Weakness

Mapping (II)

Inventory (Adventurer Special)

Spells

Minor Healing (II)

Healer's Mark (I)

Gifts

Martyr's Touch—The caster may heal oneself or others by touch and concentration, sacrificing a portion of his life to do so. Cost varies depending on the extent of the injuries healed.

Daniel could not help but sigh at his points. It was obvious he had lost quite a few points due to the use of his Gift on himself and Omrak, memories that pulled down his skill levels. He could not, for the life of him, think of why else his skills had not progressed further considering the volume of fighting they had done in the last few days. After a moment, he dismissed his usual lamentation and focused on his available Skill Point, curious to see what he would be offered.

First up, were his old choices.

Power Strike

Powerful single strike that causes additional damage to an opponent.

Skill: Active

Effect: User's Power strike does 50% more damage + 2% per level of Club skill.

Cost: 15 Stamina

Martyr's Strength

A unique skill brought about by the ongoing usage of Martyr's Touch on the individual's body. Combines an innate understanding of the owner's body with the user's unique Gift to increase regeneration rates.

Skill: Passive

Effect: User has a permanent increase of 10% to Health and Stamina regeneration.

Cost: N/A

Then, of course, were the upgrades to his existing Skills and to his Spells. But his eyes were drawn to two new options:

Titan Shield

Enhances an existing shield, expanding its size and density while reducing actual carrying weight of the affected shield. Titan Shield will also negate any single strike.

Skill: Active

Effect: Increase size and weight of existing shield by 20%. Shield may block one active attack without fail. Cooldown on active block — one hour.

Cost: 20 Stamina + 10 Mana per minute of activation

Seeing the name, Daniel could not help but sigh with envy. Titanious Domak, the great Titan. One day, Daniel swore to himself, he too would make Erlis acknowledge him and name a Skill after him.

Moderate Healing (I)

Heals minor and moderate wounds on touch.

*Effect: Heals Intelligence + 2 * Healing Skill level of wounds*

Cost: 30 Mana

Both new options greatly intrigued Daniel. His previous other major option, **Martyr's Strength**, seemed like a good choice at first — and might even be in the long-run. But on a more immediate contribution to the strength of the party, it did little. After all, a ten percent increase in regeneration might reduce the length of a bone break by a week, but it did nothing if he was bleeding to death.

On the other hand, **Titan Shield** gave him a significant upgrade to his protection. A twenty percent increase in shield size and weight did not seem like much, but the increased surface area would make covering himself easier. The increased weight would also make his **Shield Bash** skill more powerful while the single, active block option could save his life at a critical moment. As monsters grew more powerful and gained the ability to use Skills or powerful attacks, a Skill that could unerringly block those attacks made sense. Daniel could even envision how, through use of the block, he might be able to bring a badly positioned shield back into play over the long term.

But it was costly in terms of Stamina and Mana. As their healer, Daniel needed his Mana for casting spells. In fact, the Adventurer was almost afraid of running out and being unable to heal someone in need. Add the fact that a larger shield would require an adjustment in his fighting style — if nothing more than to ensure he didn't hit his own defense — and Titan Shield seemed like a Skill for another time.

Moderate Healing was almost a given that he needed to learn. Among other things, the significantly better healing ability meant that he could pull someone like Omrak back from death more quickly and efficiently. Of course, being the first level of the spell, it was touch based, unlike his upgraded **Minor Healing II**. It would require that Daniel stick closer to his party than ever to make full use of the spell during combat. But, as a Skill-developed spell, Daniel would automatically gain full mastery of the spell, allowing him to quick cast it even in the heat of battle. A not insignificant benefit.

His choice made, Daniel mentally selected the spell. A warm glow infused his mind as knowledge entered it, his Mana draining away during the process. When his Mana was half-empty, Daniel felt the drain disappear along with the knowledge gain. In his mind, now, was the full spell. With a slight flexing of his mind, he conjured the spell in his mind, watching the Mana flow to his hand and wait before he dispersed the spell. After all, no one needed healing right now.

"Daniel?" Rob said curiously, staring at Daniel's hand.

"New spell. **Moderate Healing**. Touch based," Daniel said then shot Omrak a grin. "I'll be able to fix up this lug faster."

"Ah. Complications?" Rob said.

"The usual. Don't use it too much. The spell can lead to Mana poisoning from overuse, greater resistance to healing in the future and healing-specific illnesses, diseases and mutations," Daniel said with a shrug. "It's slightly better than **Minor**

Healing for side effects but, obviously, worse than **Healer's Mark**."

"New Skill. **Cripple**," Asin piped up, flashing a grin at everyone.

"And I too," Omrak said. **"Bones of the North.** It's a defensive Skill which makes it more difficult to injure me."

"Won't that affect your rage Skill?" Daniel said with a frown.

"It will," Omrak said. "But the combination is quite common among my people for it allows us to last longer. Our Skill is not only dependent on the wounds we receive but time."

"Oh," Daniel said, acknowledging Omrak's explanation. He glanced at the team, not feeling the need to get further explanation from Asin. Her Skill choice was a common one among fighters who had high Agility and Perception. And really, unlike Omrak's flowery Skill names, Asin's Skill described what it did perfectly. "If we're ready then, we should do this."

Moments later, the group stood up, ascending the hill while Asin and Tula scampered ahead to find an appropriate location.

***

Much like the previous time they were on the second 'floor', the group lured out a patrol to deal with first. This time around, the Orcs had sent their Raptor Riders out in an attempt to run down the Tula when she fired her arrows at the archers. Luckily, Asin had been around to ambush and divert their attention, giving Tula time to make her way to the group. After that, the ambush had gone off without an issue, leaving the fort bereft of their cavalry.

Rather than repeating their mistake from earlier, the group had altered their plans for dealing with the fort. The fact that Omrak had nearly died - and quite possibly, more of them would have if he had fallen - meant that they needed to change their plans. This time around, Tula and Rob worked together to launch his enchanted poison spheres into the fort while the rest of the team waited for a reaction. They soon received one as another, larger group sortied out to chase the pair.

Rather than face the much larger, more dangerous group directly, the team continuously fell back, allowing Daniel and Tula to pepper their opponents at range. Of course, this time around, the Orcs had brought their Archers as well to the fight. Luckily, neither the Archers, Sargent or Spearmen had shields to stop the Adventurers from doing significantly more damage. Which, of course, led to them chasing the group into the waiting trap.

When the Orcs finally stumbled into the waiting Ice traps, the rest of the team attacked the broken line. Omrak charged from the side, his great sword smashing into armored torsos and leaving a trail of painful, open wounds. Asin, appearing from behind, used her **Backstab** Skill on one of the Archers before turning to the next and triggering her **Cripple** Skill. A last flurry of attacks left the Sargent reeling as she smashed the hilt of her dagger into a raised shield, cracking the shield as she triggered her **Bonecrusher** skill. Meanwhile, Tula and Rob peppered the front ranks of the Orc sortie with their ranged arrows and spells. It was only Daniel who worked to load his crossbow that did not contribute directly to the fight.

"Break!" Daniel called out as he gauged that the Orc team had recovered from their initial surprise. Asin and Omrak immediately broke from the group, Asin using her greater Agility while Omrak just hopped back before turning and running. Even as the Spearmen aimed at Omrak, Tula sent an **Arrow Storm** at his attackers, forcing them to flinch and pause. As they recovered and the Sargent barked an order to his men, Rob threw a sphere at them, this one exploding in a radiant display of colour and sound.

In moments, all but Tula and Daniel had vacated the surroundings, leaving the Orcs the choice of rushing after the fast-moving Adventurers and splitting up their group further or charging after Daniel and Tula. Both of whom were calmly loading and sending additional ranged projectiles at them.

The Sargent growled at the pair, his eyes swinging to his men as he noted that both Omrak and Asin had focused on injuring and crippling rather than killing. Other than the unfortunate Archer that Asin had backstabbed, none of the Orcs were dead. Yet.

"Go!" the Sargent yelled, pushing on the back of one of the Spearmen. In moments, the Orcs charged forwards. A moment later, the Sargent glowed and a pale-yellow light washed over the group. As a whole, the group suddenly sped up, catching Tula and Daniel by surprise.

Fortunately, the team had planned for this and a last line of defenses sprang to life. A moment later, the sped-up Orc Spearmen found themselves stumbling as the ground beneath their feet opened up, a shallow pit forming with magical speed. Rather than take advantage of the group's momentary surprise, Tula and Daniel took off, intent on leading the group to the next series of traps.

It was only a minute later that they realised that the Sargent had faked them out and pulled his people back. The moment the pair noticed this, the pair began to rush back. Even as Tula split off from Daniel, heading for a high spot that overlooked the path, Daniel could not help but grimace as he ran. Smart monsters were annoying.

Luckily, the Orcs weren't *that* smart. If they were, they might not have fallen for the initial provocation. As he jogged, Daniel could not help but wonder if it was a case of a racial issue – Orcs, even in the world above, were not known for their wisdom – or if the Dungeon itself crippled its denizens. Certainly, for a second floor of an Advanced Dungeon, these Orcs were difficult.

Idle musings were cut short soon afterwards as the Adventurer reached the quickly retreating squad of Orcs. Bending his knee, Daniel paused for a second to steady his breathing and aim as he brought the crossbow up. A cry of warning from the Orc Sargent alerted his men, but none of them stopped retreating – even when Daniel's bolt flew across the intervening distance and plunged into the leg of one of the Spearmen, hobbling him.

"Lucky." Daniel exhaled. The fact that he had been aiming for the Orc to the right of the one he hit and for a chest shot said it all. Even as he finished, Daniel reached for another bolt from the small quiver he had hung from his belt to find it empty. Unlike Tula who carried twenty arrows in her quiver, his much smaller quiver held five. After brief consideration, Daniel took the few seconds required to focus and placed his crossbow back in his Inventory before readying his hammer and shield.

"Time to get dirty," Daniel said softly to himself as he jogged to catch up. Soon enough, he saw Asin and Omrak return, the pair joining him as they raced to catch up with the group. They swiftly dispatched the lamed Orc Spearman that had been left behind, Daniel catching the Orc's spear on his shield while Omrak finished him off.

"Where's Rob?" Daniel said.

"Catching up," Omrak said with a sniff. Of course, the Enchanter, with his lower physical attributes, would be unable to keep up with the pace being set. As it was, even the three Adventurers were finding the pace set by the Orcs tough.

"Where is she?" Daniel breathed. Clad as he was in plate armor and having already run for a bit, the Adventurer found himself flagging. If it was not for the use of **Healer's Mark** to wash over some of the building fatigue, he would have fallen behind by now. As it stood, the last curve before the Orcs would be in sight of the fort was fast coming up.

As if summoned, a flock of arrows fell from the sky, landing among the surprised Orc squad. Surprised by the sudden attack, the remaining Archer fell to the ground, an arrow embedded in his shoulder. Another Orc Spearman stumbled, a pair of arrows embedded in the back of his armor. The Sargent snarled as he grabbed and shoved his men, pushing them to start running again. They took another few steps before another arrow flashed through the sky, embedding itself in the Sargent's chest armor, its tip glowing with power.

As the Sargent pitched over, the previously disciplined Spearmen stopped, their morale crumbling. A couple threw away their spears, leaving the Sargent and the remaining Spearman alone. With a yowl, Asin took off at a sprint, scrambling sideways and upwards the steep hill while Daniel and Omrak continued on the deer track. Soon, the pair found the remaining Spearman and the injured but recovered Sargent facing them.

Daniel could not help but grin, seeing the odds turn so much more favorably in their favor. Skidding to a stop a short distance away, he hefted his shield and attempted to catch his breath. His opponent saw no reason to let him rest though and shouted in anger as he rushed forward, spear levelled. Even as the pair squared off, Omrak did the same with the Sargent.

As Daniel casually blocked the spear thrust, he could not help but grin in anticipation. This was too easy.

Chapter 10

Three days later, the group stared at the imposing fort from the cover of the copse of trees. Clearing out the second fort after they had finished the squad had been simple. Their numbers significantly reduced, the group re-enacted their earlier, brazen, attack on the fort's front gate. Instead of meeting the team at the gates, the remaining Orcs had chosen to have their last stand in the fort. In either case, it changed the result very little. Once again, the party found nothing of interest in the fort itself once it was cleared, leading the group to leave and journey to this third fort.

"Anything?" Daniel asked Tula. From their vantage, they could see the way the fort front door was open and what little of the ground, empty.

"No."

"Strange," Daniel said, rubbing his chin. He looked over at his team, the group of them significantly dirtier, more tired and smellier than before. A torn sleeve here, a deeply stained pair of leather armor there were all clues to how hard fought the last few days had been. As the group journeyed deeper into the Dungeon floor, the greater the number and the fiercer the battles with the raptors had become.

And now, this.

"What do we do?" Omrak asked, fingers tapping on the hilt of his great sword.

"Scout," Asin said.

"We could use my spheres," Rob said. "I have modified the poison spheres to work with my ice enchantments. It might not be as effective, but it will still injure."

"Quiet," Asin rebutted.

"Yes, we know it's quiet," Daniel said. "It's why we're —"

"No. Quiet," Asin said, interrupting Daniel. She tapped her ears and repeated. "Quiet. Scout."

"I believe Asin speaks of her greater senses," Omrak said. "I too agree. This seems different."

"As if you can tell," Rob said with a snort. "But far be it for me to stand in the way of our suicidal scouts."

Asin flashed a tooth-filled smile at Rob before she stood up and slunk over to the fort. A long tense half hour passed before the Catkin finally made her way back.

"Gone."

"What do you mean gone?" Daniel said.

"Gone."

Daniel sighed at the lack of information but stood up to get a better view. Seeing no reaction, he waved the group to follow. As Asin blatantly strolled forwards without a care for stealth or deception, Daniel found himself following the brazen Catkin. It did not take long for them to arrive at the empty fort.

"Frost damage," Rob said as he crouched near the gate, eying the damaged wooden posts. He tilted his head to the side, peering within and staring at the scorched posts within the fort itself.

"Fire damage. Looks like a decently sized Fireball spell."

"Casey," Tula said softly, holding up the end of a broken arrow for all to see the fletching. Daniel glanced at the arrow, seeing the colourful fletching at the end and just nodded in acceptance. It was not as if he knew the difference, but obviously, the Ranger had paid attention to their rival archer's arrows.

"Magic?" Daniel said, frowning. The Fallen Leave's original team composition had not included any mages. Recalling the scene at the square in front of the Adventurers Guild, Daniel confirmed with himself that the Fallen Leaves had actually added another three members for the Dungeon. Obviously, they'd managed to fill the spots even at the last minute.

"This has been cleared by the Leaves?" Omrak said with a frown. "But why would the Dungeon send us to a cleared fort?"

"Perhaps it is not able to tell?" Tula said as she walked around the fort, eying the damage within a practised eye.

"Most likely," Rob said. "There are likely to be a set number of such forts within the second floor. One of which will contain the stairs down. It seems that it will be a matter of luck to locate the correct one."

"And it seems it takes the Dungeon some time to spawn new Orcs," Daniel said. It only took a

---

moment's more thought to realise that it made sense – after all, Artos always closed after a period of time when the Adventurers tasked with clearing it had completed their tasks. It took years before it opened up again. If the Dungeon spawned monsters at the usual rate other Dungeons did, the Dungeon would have had an outbreak every time it reopened.

Of course, that led to the question of why the Dungeon was so different from any others. But, like most questions that revolved around Dungeons, the Why continued to be a mystery.

"What now?" Rob said after a time.

Daniel paused, looking around the group and then grinned. "Well, the beds are probably still intact…"

***

A week later, the group found themselves tramping up another hill as the light above dimmed to encounter a true surprise. Seated on the hill, a fire already lit were the members of the Fallen Leaves. Casey, the Leaves' erstwhile scout had obviously, already spotted them but considered them an insufficient threat that he had to alerted the rest of his team, leaving them as surprised as Daniel's party.

"Uhhh, evening," Daniel said, greeting the group with an awkward smile.

"What are you doing here?" Gerardo said, a hand on his sword.

"We're on the way to the fort," Daniel said, pointing in the direction of the fort they had spotted.

"There's no fort there," snorted Rita. The tiny Helbing sniffed and pointed further south. "That's the fort. Are you blind?"

"No…"

"Obviously an artifact of the Dungeon's geographical manipulation," Rob said. A female in simple leather armor, quietly seated by the fire with a book before her, looked up at Rob's words. A single finger was placed in the book, keeping her place as she closed it slightly and looked over Daniel's group with more caution.

"It's warping our vision?" Omrak said with some concern.

"How did you think it was hiding the previous forts?" Rob said with a snort.

"Oh." Omrak scratched his head and then shrugged, dismissing the concern. "It seems we must share this hill tonight."

"It seems so," Gerardo said. He pointed a short distance away from their own fire. "You can set-up there."

Asin bristled slightly at Gerardo's tone but subsided as Daniel put a hand on her arm. He briefly considered suggesting that the groups share the night watch but dismissed the thought.

Somehow, he did not expect that Gerardo would be willing to entertain that notion.

"Thank you," Daniel said. The team moved to the indicated location, a simple and mostly flat place near to the other party though not too close.

By now, the team had grown used to setting up for the evening, with various members of the group dealing with the necessary evening tasks. Rob and Omrak cleared the ground of large and jagged rocks while Daniel dug a small depression in the ground and lined it with the larger rocks. He then began the tedious of starting the fire, pulling a little of the moss that he kept in a pouch out to lay the ground for the first spark. Tula and Asin moved around the clearing, quietly setting up a few, non-lethal traps to inform them if any creature attempted to sneak up on the group. Once Rob and Omrak had finished their sweep, Omrak moved off to dig a shallow latrine for the group while Rob went to collect water. Once their simple bedrolls had been laid out, Daniel had the fire going and a pot of newly located water set to boil.

"Stew again?" Tula said as she took a seat beside Daniel.

"Aye," Daniel said unrepentantly. Tula just nodded, watching as Daniel extracted some onions which he roughly chopped and tossed within, adding a couple of handfuls of barley to the stew as well to help thicken it. Simple salted meat, sliced into thin strips, had already been added as the tough protein would need the most time to soften.

140

"Do you think they'll cause trouble?" Tula said, glancing over to the other group.

"I doubt it," Daniel said. "They might not like us, but we're all Adventurers."

"Are you sure? You hear stories…" Tula trailed off, shrugging at the look Daniel gave her.

"I'm sure," Daniel said and then paused, considering. "They might not like us. Gerardo might even punch me out if he got the chance or drunk enough. But, as much as we might fight, we're all on the same side. Us Adventurers that is.

"The Dungeon – Ba'al – is our real enemy. In here, the only other person who might be willing or able to help you is another Adventurer. It's the same with miners. You might hate the bastard working next to you, but if there's a cave-in, you'll do your damnedest to pull him out. And he you."

Tula paused, considering Daniel's words before she shrugged slightly.

"Not the same in the Wilds?" Daniel said curiously.

"No." Tula shook her head. "Strangers are dangerous. You trust yourself and your friends. Those in the wild – they come for a reason. Often bad ones."

Daniel grimaced but nodded slowly. It made sense. On the edges of civilization, those who decided to travel there were often the outcasts, the brigands and those who, for one reason or another, had burnt all their bridges with 'civilized' society. The few who voluntarily chose to live on the edges often joined guilds like Tula's Western Ivy. Any who didn't were definitely suspect.

"Here, if you're going to sit. Chop up some of the mushrooms, will you?" Daniel said, reaching into his Inventory and pulling the bag of mushrooms out to hand to Tula. As she grabbed a large handful, Daniel cleared his throat. "Maybe not so many."

Tula just sighed but dropped a few down before extracting one of her knives.

***

In a few short hours, the group had bedded down on their bedrolls, having eschewed a tent. While the group had brought a few, not knowing what to expect, the lack of rain or in fact, any appreciable weather other than the ever-prevalent mists meant that the group found it more convenient and comfortable to sleep without. As Daniel slowly walked the perimeter of their camp, keeping his gaze pointed at the deep darkness that lay outside the camp, he could not help but glance over at the other team's camp.

In truth, the Fallen Leaves' camp looked little different from theirs. A single campfire lit the encampment, the group bedded down around the source of warmth with weapons close at hand while a single other scout walked the perimeter.

Curious, Daniel stared at his fellow guard, a newcomer to the Fallen Leaves.

Tall, broad, with a chiselled jaw and a scar that ran along his neck, the guard looked to be in his early twenties like Daniel himself. He was clad in an interesting layered armor, one made of numerous riveted together portions that gleamed slightly in the light. Earlier, in the fading evening light, Daniel had noted the strange armor looked almost like scales, but more uniform and rectangular. On his hips, the man wore a pair of knives and a short sword, an easy indicator of the man's dual-wielding fighting style. But both those melee weapons lay sheathed, replaced by a large, cocked crossbow.

Seeing Daniel's interested gaze, the guard smiled and walked over, the crossbow cradled in his arms. Daniel tensed slightly before he chided himself – there was no reason to think the other Adventurer would hold the same animosity as the original Fallen Leaves.

"Daniel isn't it? Eiju Walnar," Eiju greeted Daniel, offering his hand. Daniel took it, absently noting the strength the other Adventurer showed. On closer inspection, Daniel could also see a small pin which gleamed red, showcasing a burning field which was placed near his throat.

"You're a Burning Field member?" Daniel said.

"Yes," Eiju said. "And you're unaligned."

"I was wondering…"

"About my armor. It's steel, with a leather underlayer. But the shine comes from lacquer," Eiju said.

"Lacquer?"

"A sap from a tree. Similar to wax in many ways, but harder," Eiju said, pausing. "It protects the steel from the rain."

"Of course," Daniel said. Rust was a pain, especially in humid weather like this. Even in the best circumstances, his armor was constantly stained with the internal fluids from the monsters he killed. It was an annoying fact that since the blood and other viscera spilled on him came into close contact with his aura, they persisted long after said monster had died. Persisted sufficiently to rust his plate mail, which Daniel then had to scrub off. "Would it…?"

"Probably. Though, it is expensive to add and does require constant care. Just in a different manner," Eiju said. Daniel's face fell slightly which made Eiju chuckle. "The armor is much lighter though. Of course, the scale mail is less useful against blunt attacks like your hammer."

"So, are all the rest? …" Daniel glanced back to the Fallen Leaves and the sleeping forms.

"Yes, they will, if they do not fail, join the Fields. This Dungeon will be a trial run for the Leaves. Of course, it wouldn't be fair without a healer, so myself, Kelly and Camilo are here to even out the numbers. And ensure the new would-be recruits don't die."

"You're that good?" Daniel said softly, cocking his head to the side. Certainly, Eiju had a certain presence to him that he only felt from older, more experienced Adventurers.

"We are. We were, unfortunately, too late to join the arena fight or else you'd have seen it for yourself. A Quest took us out of the city before the announcement," Eiju said and then shrugged, dismissing the matter.

"They offered me a place…" Daniel muttered, thinking to himself. Not that he hadn't been offered a chance to join the Fields either. He still struggled with the fact that he had turned them down – but his Gift, his secret was too dangerous to simply share.

"Only fools complain about having more healers," Eiju replied with a grin. "And for all his temper, Gerardo is no fool."

"Just angry," Daniel said unhappily.

"Well, you did take his spot," Eiju said. "And ours."

"But you're not angry about it," Daniel pointed out.

"We're here, aren't we?" Eiju said with a shrug. "And I have to admit, I'm a little impressed. Turning down the Fields and kicking us out of our spot is something few can brag about. Or would."

"I didn't…"

"Yes, yes. You didn't mean to. But it was done."

Daniel sighed, realising that for all his initial friendliness, Eiju did hold a little grudge. Or perhaps he was just this patronising in general.

"Did you find any empty forts?" Daniel asked, deciding to change topics.

"A few," Eiju confirmed. "We've cleared seven so far."

"Six."

"The Champion?"

"No. For either floor."

"Ah, we cleared this floor's Champion two days ago." Daniel flinched at the words, the movement making Eiju smile just a little. "A challenging fight. Strong. And big."

"How big?" Daniel's curiosity prompted him to ask.

"About thrice the size of your average raptor."

Daniel winced again, imagining the size of the creature. Being bitten by that monster could be instantly lethal.

"I'm glad none of you were killed."

"Thank you." Eiju bobbed his head and then glanced away from the Adventurer before adding, "We should continue our rounds. No use being on watch if we stand in the same spot, talking."

"Aye," Daniel acknowledged. "Good night."

As Eiju walked away, Daniel could not help but sigh. Damn it. They needed to speed up. He would not let the Leaves walk away with both Champion's Mana Stones.

***

Over breakfast the next day, Daniel related what he had learnt to the rest of the team. By the time his own group were ready to leave, the Fallen Leaves had packed and left, moving quickly towards 'their' fort.

"No more hills except at night. We pick the direction and we keep going till we get to the next fort," Daniel said. "We only ascend the hills at night."

The group shared a long look, each member of the party testing each other's resolve. Seeing no one flinch away from the much harder and difficult journey ahead, Daniel waved Tula onward.

"Let's find that Champion."

Chapter 11

Two weeks. Two weeks of travelling from fort to fort, increasingly finding the buildings already raided and empty. Even the raptor attacks had begun to decrease as the teams slowly cleared the floor, killing the monsters that roamed the mist-enshrouded lower valleys. Journey's between the forts had sped up since the reduction in ambushes, allowing the team to visit and clear ever more locations.

But now, they finally had found the likely end of the second floor. In front of them loomed a much larger, more imposing fort. Rather than the short, ten-foot wooden walls they had defeated previously, this fort was made of stone with walls twenty feet in the air and set against the hill it had been built on. The fort itself was twice the size of what they had dealt with from what they could make out, and it could easily have been larger behind the rooms they could see.

All of which meant that the team was taking the matter much more seriously, having hidden in a nearby copse of trees. That this caution had been warranted was clear as they watched a second mounted patrol ride past them. For a time, silence pervaded the trees as the patrol moved on and the team waited.

"Here," Tula said softly as she neared the group. A moment later, the bushes parted and the Ranger stepped through, offering a quick nod to her team. Fingers relaxed and weapons were set aside when the Ranger was positively confirmed. Rather than continue speaking, the Ranger led the team down the hill, away from the roving patrols. Only when they were at the edges of the boundary of the next floor did Tula speak. "Four Archers. One patrol of six Riders. Shift change every six hours."

"Two? Three? Four groups?" Daniel said, mulling over the numbers as he spoke. A shift changes every six hours could mean an on-off schedule for two groups, but that made little sense. More likely either three or four sets of guards. Which meant... "twelve or sixteen Archers? And eighteen or twenty-four Riders. And an unknown number of Spearmen. But, at the old ratios — another forty or so Spearmen?"

"That seems about right, though your numbers are likely low for the Spearmen," Rob said.

"That's impossible," Daniel said. Sure, the Orcs were individually much weaker than each Adventurer. Even Rob could hold his own against an Archer. Between the increased teamwork, fluidity of their tactics and knowledge of the Orcs habits, the group were much more competent than before. In fact, Daniel was sure, they could take on a small fort directly now and win. But that was against fourteen or fifteen Orcs in total. Not four times that number.

"We must split them," Omrak stated. "An ambush or two on their patrols would reduce those numbers."

"Surprised a Northerner is fine with ambushes. Not very honorable is it?" Rob said with a sniff.

"Honorable?" Omrak frowned then gave Rob a wide grin. "Oh, but you forget. That's how we win against your kingdom. Ambushes are a time-honored tactic to win against a more numerous opponent."

Rob sniffed but said nothing while Daniel stared back towards the fort. "Ambushes are good. Dealing with the patrol individually is fine. But what if they send the other patrols after us?"

His words caused the others in the group to fall silent. If the Orcs sent a second Raptor Rider party immediately from the fort, the team would be hard pressed to win. If the fort then added an infantry squad as additional reinforcements, unless they could beat the Riders quickly, they would be unable to disengage. At which point, they'd be fighting at least twenty or twenty-five Orcs. And the raptors.

After looking around for a second, Daniel moved over to a bare earthen area and squatted down, quickly sketching a rough map of the fort and its surroundings. Tula joined him soon afterwards, squatting beside him and adding a few noteworthy terrain features. With a sweep of his hand, Daniel added a line to indicate the boundary of the Riders patrol before he stared at the rough map.

"Can we do this?" Daniel said, slowly tracing a route with his finger down from one section to another, a route that led past a series of boulders which lay next to a small steam. Not deep enough to stop one from wading through, but sufficient to slow.

"No," Tula said, shaking her head and pointed. "Path, here. Raptors would ride us down."

"Ah…"

As Daniel went back to staring at the map, the group gathered around, tossing out suggestions of their own. For all the flaws in the ambush tactic, it was the only viable one they had.

****

They began the ambush when the patrol was at the furthest point from the entrance of the fort. An **Arrow Storm** from the hidden Tula showered the Raptor Riders, injuring and alerting the group. As the team had feared, the lead rider immediately raised a horn to his lips, blowing on it to signal the fort. For his troubles, the horn-blower received an arrow his throat, causing him to tumble to the ground clutching at his neck.

As the patrol charged towards her hiding spot, Tula turned and ran into the underbrush, ducking around the sparse trees. The agile raptors followed after her, clawed toes digging into the soft earth as they strode to catch their elusive prey. Breathing heavily, bow clutched tight in her hand, Tula ran without looking back, trusting in her team.

"Another!" shouted a Rider, short moments before Asin's throwing knives pierced his breastplate. As the enchanted lightning from her bracers shocked the Orc, it stiffened and fell off the raptor which skidded to a stop in confusion. When the monster's eyes alighted on Asin's form, it hissed and dashed forwards, intent on injuring its owner's attacker. Asin, on the other hand, calmly cocked her hand back and threw another knife, engaging **Fan of Knives** as she did so. The newly created series of blades clattered against the tough scaled hide of the raptor, but a pair managed to lodge between the scales in the chest and throat. Yet the damage was insufficient to stop the raptor, forcing Asin to jump behind a convenient tree before rushing off. Attracted by the first Rider's shout, another Raptor Rider peeled off the main group and angled his mount to ride down the now-fleeing Catkin.

All this, Tula managed to glimpse while running. The path she had been on had curved slightly, offering her the opportunity to watch Asin separate the Riders. Knowing her part in the plan, Tula risked one quick glance back and confirmed that the remaining three riders and four raptors were directly behind her. As she looked back, she saw the lone rope hanging down in the middle of the path. Bunching her legs beneath her, the

Ranger threw herself at the rope and swung across the ground, using the momentum of the rope to carry her around the corner.

Of course, those strange actions would be enough to scare the Riders. Rather than risk running into a likely pit trap, the group pulled to a hasty stop, the raptors skidding and sliding on the leaf-strewn earth.

"Now!" a voice called as the group came to a standstill. From above, a net dropped, entangling a pair of Riders and their raptors. Moments later, small spheres filled with enchanted ice traps were tossed into the center of the group to freeze and slow the monsters. Along with the attacks, a hatchet and a bolt flew from either side of the trail, crushing and skewering the unridden raptor.

"Die!" Omrak roared as he charged out, his sword gripped in his free hand as the Orcs struggled to free themselves. Daniel dropped his crossbow as well, taking to the trail as he pulled his hammer from his belt and crashed into the entangled pair with his shield to throw them off.

In the midst of the fight, Tula continued running, headed for her next vantage point. As the mad scramble on the trail filled with the crunch of broken bones and the cries of bleeding creatures, Daniel prayed that they had timed this right.

"Slaves!" the Raptor Rider spat as he lay on the ground, one leg crushed under his fallen ride and an arm shattered, blood spilling from the bone shard sticking out. The muscular Orc – sporting a surprisingly full and well-coiffed beard – glared at Daniel as the Adventurer raised his hammer one last time. For a brief second, Daniel hesitated before he brought the hammer down.

"What was that about?" Daniel panted out while looking about him at the slain. The last word, it had been disturbing in a way that he was not certain he liked.

Omrak ignored Daniel's words, turning towards the fast approaching sound of a pair of raptors. In seconds, Asin burst from the trees, the remaining members of the Orc patrol on her heels.

"Down," Omrak commanded the Catkin who promptly dropped and rolled. Her movements allowed her to narrowly dodge a snapping mouth even as the raptor skidded to the side under the guidance of its rider. Leaning over the side, the Rider raised its sabre to lash out at the recovering Beastkin. Behind him, the final raptor rushed Asin from her other side.

Before they could finish the attack, Omrak channelled the small build-up of rage he had achieved into Asin's attackers. The bolts of lightning reached out, stabbing into the riders and raptors. As the Orc and the raptors recovered, Daniel plowed into them with his shield, using his greater mass and lower centre of gravity to bowl the pair over. After that, finishing the remaining members of the squad was simple.

"Let's go," Daniel commanded the group when the last raptor fell under Asin's knives. Any thoughts about the previous Orc's words were gone under the flurry of combat. Daniel's friends nodded in return, and together the trio rushed off into the undergrowth.

***

Tula growled softly as she ran, finding the small hill that she had scouted and clambering up its steep slope. Squatting down, she struggled to control her breathing as she looked down towards the abundant vegetation. Thankfully, they were high enough that the low-lying mists that covered the valleys were mostly gone. Unfortunately, the vegetation blocked most of her view. Most.

There.

She quickly pulled and set a trio of arrows down next to her before picking one up and setting it to her bow. The Ranger did not draw yet, instead watching the moving vegetation that marked the advance of the Orc reinforcements. Letting her eyes track further backwards, Tula grimaced as she caught sight of the slow-moving infantry crossing the cleared zone that demarcated the no man's land in front of the walls. Unlike the smaller forts, the cleared ground before the walls was sufficient that even Tula's powerful recurve would have trouble reaching the walls from the safety of the trees.

The presence of both the infantry and cavalry reinforcements was nearly the worst possibility that the group had planned for. If they were not able to slow down the cavalry, it was quite likely that none of the others would be able to escape. Stakes well in mind, Tula drew the arrow to her cheek and focused, exhaling threadedly once and heavily before she loosed the arrow.

The arrow spun through the air, darting through vegetation and disappearing from sight. Tula did not hesitate, picking and firing the second arrow at the same location, adjusting just slightly. The vegetation was dense enough that she could only guess at where the Orc Riders were going to be. If she managed to actually injure any of her opponents, it would be a miracle.

But that was not the point.

Swiftly, Tula picked up the last arrow and waited. Already, she could see how the flashes of black skin and brown leather armor had shifted, the way the vegetation now moved towards her. A slight smile flickered across her face even as the low chanting from the newly arrived, slightly breathless Enchanter beneath her stand reached her ears.

Good.

She released the arrow, this time imbuing the arrow with her **Arrow Storm** skill. She watched as the arrows shredded the vegetation ahead of her, a lucky arrow even managing to embed itself in the arm of a raptor.

Job done, Tula turned and ran up the hill and down the other side even as she drew another arrow from her quiver. For a second, Tula thought she saw movement at the boundaries of the forest in front of the walls but dismissed it from her mind. Now was the time to run. Now, it was all up to Rob.

***

"-ima ja lars!" Rob spat out and exhaled, staring at the frost-rimed, rock-strewn ground. He eyed it for a second more and then withdrew a couple more of his enchanted spike traps, casually tossing them among the rocks after turning on their trigger with a surge of Mana.

"I should have demanded an extra share," Rob muttered to himself as he turned around to run back. As he neared the forest, he took a light hop, jumping over the yellow flowers that had spread across the smaller ground. As he landed, he felt his foot sink into the ground more deeply and he made a face, feeling the mud squish.

"Outdoors. Why did this Dungeon have to be outdoors?" Rob complained to no one. If not for the fact that Tula continually glared at those who made noise, Rob knew he would have been content to make more noise. Not as much as

Omrak, of course, but he found no reason to hold back now. It wasn't as if it was actually a problem if the raptors came after him.

So long as Daniel and the rest of the team actually finished their targets off in time.

If not, well.

Rob fingered his necklace again. It was not as if he and his Master had not planned for such an eventuality. It would be a shame to fail at the Dungeon, but his life was significantly more important than some stupid directive by the Adventurers Guild.

And as for his team, well. They were Adventurers. They knew the risk.

Screams and hissing screeches erupted from behind Rob as he jogged along the track. Already, the Enchanter could feel his breath growing shorter, a stitch beginning in his side. Rather than suffer through it, Rob reached into a pouch and pulled forth a small purplish-yellow potion, downing the bottle in one quick rush. Seconds later, he felt energy rush through his body, allowing him to pick up the pace again.

Better living through alchemy.

Now, which way would the Riders go?

***

Crouched behind the boulders next to the stream, Omrak fingered the edge of the throwing axe once again. Waiting was always the most difficult part of an ambush, especially a multi-stage ambush like this one. Running from place to place with short, explosive fights in-between had the tendency to increase his heart rate and adrenaline in short-bursts. It required discipline and experience to control otherwise…

"Stop!" Asin snapped at Omrak as she sniffed at the air.

Omrak grimaced, pulling his thumb back from the bloody throwing axe and sucking on the wound. The Beastkin's senses were incredibly sharp to notice the blood he had shed already by pushing too hard. Still, after a time, Omrak took his thumb out of his mouth where it crept, unconsciously, towards the axe's edge. It stopped only when the Catkin straightened.

"Coming?" Omrak said.

"Yes." Asin nodded. She shot a glance down towards Daniel who nodded and began the laborious process of loading his crossbow. Her hand twitched slightly, pulling a pair of throwing knives from her Inventory before the Beastkin subsided once more.

"How many?" Omrak said. Could she tell? He was never sure exactly how much the Catkin could sense. A shrug was all he received and Omrak sighed. Well, it did not matter. Not really.

"HELP!" Rob came crashing out from the forest, a panicked look on his face as he raced down the minor slope that edged the stream. In seconds, Rob assessed his location and shifted directions slightly, heading for the series of rocks further upstream that would allow him to cross the stream. Unfortunately for the Enchanter, hot on his heels were the members of the cavalry patrol.

"Daniel…" Omrak whispered, eyeing the distances. From Omrak's estimation, there was no way for the Enchanter to make the stream before the raptors got to him.

"Ba'al!" Daniel cursed and then stood up. Taking their leader's cue, the pair stood as well and together, the trio of Adventurers loosed their ranged attacks across the stream at the cavalry patrol.

Once again pandemonium ensued as magically created knives, a throwing axe and a badly aimed crossbow bolt landed among the closely bunched group of raptor riding orcs. Working from a shared understanding built from years working together, Daniel and Omrak left the lead raptor to Asin, the pair targeting the second-in-line. Of course, Daniel's shot winged right past the rider's shoulder to bury itself in a tree further back, but Omrak's throwing axe buried itself in its leg.

Taking the moment of confusion offered by his friends, Rob hopped, skipped and jumped across the stream before he managed to make it across with a wet boot and no injuries. Rob did not stop, however, angling towards the trio of Adventurers. Omrak chuckled as threw another axe, watching this one be deflected from the air by a well-timed cut.

For a time, the Raptor Rides fought for control of their mounts before a barked command from their leader had the group wheel around. Omrak's last throwing axe flew, embedding itself in the back of one of the retreating Orcs, sending the Orc tumbling off his raptor before the group rode away.

"Nooo!" Daniel cursed as he leveled his finally-recocked crossbow at the swaying branches. Cursing, he shifted the aim of his crossbow bolt, sending it spiraling into the back of the unraptored Orc. The bolt sank low into its back, sending the Orc stumbling to the ground. As it struggled back upwards, a **Magic Arrow** and a throwing knife ended its life.

"That was all of them, right?" Daniel said, eyeing the swaying vegetation.

"Yes. None of them followed Tula," Rob said. "She should be fine."

"Then we should go. Before the rest of the reinforcements arrive," Daniel said, waving the group. Quickly, the group assembled and took off jogging, headed for the next rally point. While not finishing off the second cavalry group was a failure, no one was injured. Which was, in the end, the best result they could wish for. Now, all they had to do was come up with a new plan to deal with the remainder of the Orcs.

Chapter 12

A day later, the team slowly made their way back to the fort. When they arrived at the lookout point they had chosen, Tula was already waiting and frowning.

"What's wrong?" Daniel asked softly.

"No cavalry," Tula said. "Gates are damaged."

"Damaged?"

Tula nodded and pointed. Daniel squinted but could not see any difference, eventually giving up. Without Tula's Skill, details at this range were just not possible. Even for the Ranger, it was obvious that she was straining by the little frown on her face.

"What kind of damage?" Rob said.

Tula shrugged and Daniel tapped his fingers, wondering what else they should do. Asin, looking between the group, suddenly stiffened and turned her head sideways, sniffing slightly. Her tail lashed, Omrak immediately tensing as he shifted in the direction that Asin looked, a hand dropping to the hilt of his sword. A brief moment later Asin relaxed slightly, her tail stopping its jerky movement.

"Leaves." Asin pointed downwind.

"The Leaves? Why would…" At this point, Rob fell silent before he sighed. "Taking the time to set-up our traps took too long. They caught up."

"Yesterday, I saw a flash," Tula admitted quietly. "It must have been them. They probably attacked the fort while we distracted the others."

"But that gate's still closed," Omrak said.

"So they didn't succeed?" Daniel said, a rising note of hope in his voice. "Then, we still have a chance."

"Of what?" Rob said caustically. "There are still over fifty Orcs in there, at least."

Rob's words brought silence to the group once again. With the gates closed and the Archers on the walls, approaching would be difficult at best. After two weeks of fighting, even Tula's overstocked Traveller's Pouch had begun to run low on her arrows. A long-range duel was out of the question, especially considering there was another floor left.

"We can work with the Leaves," Daniel finally said.

"Why would they work with us?" Omrak said.

"Their failure at breaching the gate might offer some reason," Rob said.

"Ah, an alliance of convenience?" Omrak nodded. "But the Champion…?"

"Is something we'll deal with when we talk to them," Daniel said firmly. After the group slowly nodded, he looked at Asin who flashed a grin, slinking off in the direction of the smell.

***

"You can come out now," Rita called out. A few moments later, Asin exited the foliage with the rest of the team, waving a hand in greeting. The group just looked at her and the rest of the team flatly.

"Afternoon," Daniel said. "Asin noticed you were here."

"As did we with your little stunt," Gerardo said. Left unsaid was the fact that the Leaves had seen fit not to meet with them.

"We saw the damage on the gates," Daniel said. "It seems they've withdrawn into the fort for now."

"For now," Gerardo said. "They will come out."

"And if they don't?" Daniel asked.

"Then we go in," Rita said with a shrug and grin. "Sneaking into a big place like that isn't hard."

"For you. And Asin. But how about the rest of us?" Daniel said, shaking his head. "There's no way we're going to make it up without attracting attention. And then we'd be finding over forty Orcs."

"Forty-eight," Eiju said. Gerardo growled but the melee fighter just smiled back. "There are other ways to deal with them, but they are all risky. Working with DAO is our best bet."

"I still don't like that name," Tula muttered.

"We will not work with those backstabbing, Orc-loving, sheep-swilling degenerates!" Casey said.

"You shouldn't hold back on what you think, Casey," Rita said with a laugh in her voice.

Farhad just stared at the group, his gaze flat. Behind him, the female in the light armor looked between the group, sniffed and returned back to her reading while the other, a fully armed and armored spearman worked on the edge of his spear as he sat next to the mage. Obviously, the two newcomers from the Field had little concern about the argument.

"We didn't choose…" Daniel caught himself and paused, forcing himself to exhale breathily to calm himself. He was not going to defend himself again. "You don't have to like us. But we're just on the second floor here and it's been over two weeks. Erlis knows how big the third floor is going to be. We can either work together or sit around and pray that the Orcs decide to stop hiding before our rations run out."

"Then we wait," Gerardo said, crossing his arms.

"Such a logical and well-thought-out plan," Rob said with a snort.

"You know, my bow arm is getting tired," Casey said, idly twitching the bow he held in his hand.

"It's not even draw-" Omrak stopped as the Fallen Leaves archer drew back on his bow, an arrow nocked.

"Go," Asin said softly and turned, walking off.

Daniel stared at the group one last time before he finally spoke. "We'll be waiting."

***

Over breakfast a few days later, Daniel quizzed Asin and Tula. Obviously, they were not going to just wait for something to happen which was they had been watching the fort. Last night, Asin and Tula had been tasked with the objective of sneaking into the fort and seeing what they could learn.

"Hard. Patrols walls. Five minutes. Torches lit. Everywhere," Asin said, ticking her fingers off. "Raptors in courtyard. Smell."

"Did you manage to sneak in at all?" Daniel said, frowning. He knew that the majority of the night had been spent getting the pair close to the wall itself. And of course, getting back before 'day' began.

"Little. Gate barred. No portcullis," Asin said. "Stables for raptors. Half out," she added then shook her head. "Left fast."

"Sounds like sneaking us in would be difficult," Rob chimed in. Daniel had to nod, thinking about the tall wall. If the patrols came by every five minutes, getting the whole team up the wall and to a quiet, hidden place would be impossible. Especially if the courtyard was being guarded by raptors.

"Any place to hold on the wall?" Daniel asked next. After further questioning and short, somewhat cryptic answers from Asin, Daniel discarded the idea of holding a building or other fortification in the fort. There were no towers on the wall to enter and secure and Daniel was unwilling to risk entering any of the smaller stand-alone buildings inside the walls. After all, if they could not defeat the Orcs, they would have no retreat.

"Well, what next, Mr. Lee?" Rob said, arms crossed over his body. With breakfast finished, the team sat around the low fire, wondering what to do. Well, all but Omrak who sat above them to watch for potential trouble.

"I'm not sure," Daniel said. This was a siege situation, and he was not a general. It was not as though being a miner had offered much knowledge in siege tactics. While he mulled the topic over, Asin broke into a toothy yawn and pointed to her bedroll.

"Go ahead. You too, Tula. And thank you," Daniel said.

"For what?" Tula said and slinked off dispiritedly. Daniel watched the Ranger for a moment but chose not to say anything comforting — after all, he knew how she felt. Staring at the fort, day in and day out, being unable to do anything was dispiriting. Especially for Adventurers like them who were more used to action.

Daniel fell silent for a time, pondering their options. With a quick movement, he unrolled a map that he had drawn of the surroundings, looking at the details once again. As much as he hated to admit it, the fort before them was a significant issue. Outnumbered as they were, they could not attack it directly. The occupants of the fort itself did not need to leave – they were not a guard or a projection of force, unlike real kingdoms. Even the thought of depriving the Dungeon residents of water might be problematical. Dungeon creatures did not necessarily procure their nourishment as normal but subsisted on the Mana fed into them via the Mana stone in their bodies.

In any normal Dungeon run, the solution to this perplexing problem would be simple. The Adventurers would leave, coming back another time to clear more raptors and Orcs in other locations until they gained sufficient strength to face the Dungeon fort directly. Or perhaps they would purchase the necessary equipment to do so – repeating crossbows, a large quantity of area of effect enchantments, maybe oil and fire to burn the courtyard down. There were sure to be a significant number of situations to the problem, but none of them were available to them right this second.

Which, perhaps, Daniel considered, was the point of the Dungeon. Sometimes, you just had to make do with what you had. Even if the Dungeon was an artificial construct, the clergy of Panqua often reiterated that his actions were to strengthen humanity. A Dungeon that was too easy would be the opposite of that.

Of course, none of that helped Daniel find a solution.

"We are graced with company," Omrak said calmly. As the giant was not reaching for his sword, it was clear that the company was friendly. And in this Dungeon, friendly obviously meant the Fallen Leaves.

Soon enough, the members of the Fallen Leaves could be seen. Daniel was somewhat surprised to see that the entire team was here, a fact that put the healer slightly on guard. If they were here to talk, it seemed a little extravagant to bring everyone.

"Mr. Chai?" Gerardo said, stomping up to Daniel and stopping before him.

"Gerardo." Daniel inclined his head. "Fallen Leaves."

"I do not like this, but it seems we have little choice. I do not agree with your methods or your presence here, but we have a job to do," Gerardo said.

"Wasn't that what we said earlier?" Tula whispered not so quietly to Asin. The yawning Catkin who had just managed to bed down could only nod while Gerardo's face tightened briefly at the Ranger's words before he allowed it to relax.

"Will you work with us?" Gerardo said.

"Yes, of course!" Daniel replied, smiling. He offered his hand but dropped it after a moment when Gerardo made no move to take it.

"Then let us begin. Rita and Asin will be required for the initial assault. Tula and Casey will provide cover fire at the northeast…" Gerardo said, striding forwards and using the tip of his sword to point to the locations he spoke of on the map that Daniel had been poring over. Gerardo barked out orders while the Adventurers moved to listen.

All the while, Daniel gritted his teeth. While the other party was more experienced, they were no slouches either. Yet, in light of the sudden change in attitude and the need to clear the Dungeon, Daniel kept his mouth shut. His ego could take a little snubbing, so long as the plan was safe.

And if not, well, then he would object.

***

Running alongside Tula and Casey, Daniel had his mace held alongside his body and shield held to the front at the ready. A part of him was truly regretting not taking the Titan Shield Skill right about then, especially considering his current role. But, if wishes were stones, everyone would be king. On the opposite side, the silent dark-skinned spearman – Camilo - ran beside Casey, his spear held loosely in one hand as he carried a large kite shield with the other.

"Here!" Casey barked, and Tula and he skidded to a stop. Moving as though they had practised the motions, the pair withdrew a half dozen arrows and stabbed them into the ground. Even as the archers readied themselves, Daniel and Camilo strode forwards and placed their bodies ahead and to the side of the archers, their shield at the ready. Not even their fast advance was sufficient to keep the Orcs surprised forever, and arrows began to fall around the group.

"Ready?" Casey asked. Tula just raised her bow slightly, arrow already nocked.

"Loose!" Daniel swung his shield aside at the command, opening the way for Tula. The Ranger quickly sighted and loosed her arrow even as Daniel swung his shield back into place. He noted absently that one of the Archers above was huge, larger than the rest. Not a moment too soon as an arrow slammed into his shield, making the healer grunt.

"Ready."

"Loose!"

In time, the group got into the rhythm of the attack as arrows landed around the group. Each time Daniel shifted the shield away, he took the time to look at the gate, waiting. Even as the arrow fire intensified as more archers arrived, Daniel could not help but glance at the gates.

A long beat, a pause and another three arrows landed. Casey's lips peeled back into a wolfish grin, the Adventurer having anticipated the Orcs own judgement of their timing.

"Loose!"

Again, arrows flew and a shield slammed back into place. A stifled grunt from the side caught Daniel's attention. By the side, Casey continued squatting while the edge of an arrow sat beside his leg, having scraped the side of his body before ending its flight.

"Ready!"

"Loose!"

Daniel snorted slightly as the loud creaking of uncared for hinges informed him of the opening of the gates. No need to pay attention, even a sleeping dragon would wake from that racket.

"Up! We retreat together," Casey ordered. Tula swiftly stood, snatching three arrows into her bow hand another two to fit to her bow. At Casey's look, she drew the arrows to her cheek, awaiting his command.

"Loose."

Arrows spun through the air, the three arrows flashing through the sky towards the grouped archers. Tula engaged **Arrow Storm** immediately, making her arrows double, her face paling as the Skill drained her Mana and Stamina. Beside her, Casey's enchanted arrow hummed as it flew, a shriek that grew in pitch and sent the opposing archers to clutching their ears. Daniel risked a glance towards the gates where the cavalry had just begun to ride out.

"Back!" Casey took a step back, his motion followed by Camilo immediately. Tula and Daniel were less co-ordinated, but together, the group slowly backed off. A loud crack echoed through the field a moment later followed by a wash of hot air, dirt and leaves.

"What was that?" Daniel said, forcing himself not to rub at his eyes.

"Kelly," Camilo said with a grin.

"Loose!" Daniel snapped his shield aside again. At the front of the gates was a small hole which the cavalry fought to control their raptors around. Beside the hole, Daniel could see the still forms of raptors and Orcs while even more bled from injuries.

Automatically, Daniel brought the shield back to cover Tula. As he stepped back, he felt the hard rap of an arrow landing flush on his leg armor before the pain arrived. A look down indicated that the arrow had embedded itself, but the pain told him it was not deep. Resolutely, Daniel ignored the matter, forcing himself to take another step back with the group.

He just hoped that the rest of the plan was going well.

***

"What a powerful spell," Rob said, stroking his slick beard. He eyed Kelly, the Burning Field's mage, who smiled wanly at him. It was obvious, even to the untrained, uncultured Adventurers, that this was not a spell that she could cast often. As Rob eyed the results, he mentally added – or accurately.

"They're regrouping," Omrak, standing beside Rob, growled. The big Northerner's eyes flashed between the small retreating party of archers and the now re-organised cavalry and added. "They won't make it in time."

"No one expected them to," Gerardo said with a sniff. Beside the Leaves' leader, Farhad just stared at Omrak before he went back to staring, hands on the hilts of his sword. "Not without help."

Omrak huffed but fell silent for which Rob was only thankful. The big Northerner could be annoyingly loud at times, and right now, silence was required. If nothing more than to give him the time to concentrate on his own spell. It would be embarrassing to be so completely upstaged by another Mage.

Admittedly, **Mana Manipulation** was not exactly a spell. It was a Skill which gave him greater control of his Mana than most Mages. In particular, the Skill allowed him to extend the threads of Mana that he wove into the middle of the field. There, he began to weave **Magic Arrow**, once, twice and then again, stopping at the last junction for each.

"Now!" Gerardo called. Not that Rob required the signal. Pushing one last time on the Mana, the spells snapped into place, forming in the middle of the field and firing forwards and upwards. Directly into the bodies of three different raptors. Only a last moment jerk by a raptor saved it, leaving two injured creatures and one unraptored rider.

Once again, the cavalry group was thrown into disarray as they searched for their hidden attacker. Even as Rob began to smirk, Omrak spoke.

"Second cavalry group," Omrak said.

Gerardo cursed. The Orcs were moving faster than expected. Worse, there was a Raptor Rider in the second who wore leather armor with purple highlights and rode a larger than normal raptor, waving his arm to command the other group. It was not possible to see the details about the Raptor Rider at this range, but instinct told Rob that the rider was not a normal one.

Even the initial group of cavalry riders had regained their sense of balance, willing to rush the group down. This was the danger of setting up an archer duel – getting caught in the open field by the cavalry, being forced to fight uneven odds. All the while being pinned down by the archers on the walls.

"Are we ready?" Gerardo called, eyeing the distance between Daniel's group and the treeline. Too far for them to make it to the trees. If they rushed out to help, the entire group might be in danger. As the raptors shrieked and rode towards Daniel, Rob licked his lips in dry-mouthed anticipation.

Chapter 13

Asin pulled herself up on the wall, dropping down onto the wooden rampart and keeping low. For a moment, she stayed tense as she listened for cries of outrage or any other acknowledgement that the Orcs had noticed them. Rita, already on the walkway shook her head, waving the Catkin along.

Keeping her body bent, Asin ran along beside the Helbing, the tiny Adventurer not even needing to duck to stay hidden. It was a somewhat unfair advantage for these kinds of activities. Considering the pair were running along the rampart directly above the boiling mass of Orc infantry, Asin could not help but wish that she be that small.

Together, the pair continued their run, rushing around the wall to the side where the archers had clustered. Lousy discipline or overconfidence, in either case, the rest of the wall was currently empty. Even as they ran, they could hear the screams, grunts and clash of battle from the field. A quick glance as she ran informed Asin that the initial cavalry group had managed to catch Daniel's group, hemming the group in as they rode around and the archers continued to pepper the stalled team.

Asin found herself snarling and inadvertently speeding up. If they did not get into position soon, the Adventurers would die. Her longer legs at first allowed her to overtake Rita, but the Helbing put on a burst of speed, coming side by side with Asin in the next moment. In seconds, the pair were near the archer line where Asin noted the larger than normal Archer and the prettier than normal bow.

A look was sufficient for its status information to come to her.

Orc Archer Sargent (Level 14)
Health: 170/170

Together, the pair of Adventurers hit the Archer line without warning. Rather than using her throwing knives, Asin wielded her long daggers, darting through the group as she triggered her Skills one after the other. **Backstab**, **Cripple**, **Bone breaker**. Each one used on a new Archer, each blow crippling and throwing the group in disarray even as the lightning aura from her enchanted bracers added their own dosage of pain.

Beside her, Rita attacked as well. The smaller Adventurer dual-wielded a pair of knives which were large enough to be short swords in her hands. Using them, she struck at unarmored lower bodies, slicing Achilles, hamstrings and sliding the blades along their inner thighs. Each attack left sickly green skin, veins and arteries almost immediately darkening as Rita's **Poisonous Sting** Skill took effect.

Confusion and pain. The Archers reacted slowly, surprised by the sudden appearance of the pair of Adventurers in their midst. As she neared the Archer Sargent, he swung his bow at Asin who dropped sideways, letting one hand land on the ground to prop herself up as her feet bunched against the nearby wall. A moment later, after the strike had passed above her head, Asin kicked off the wall and threw her weight against her attacker. The Sargent staggered for a second, recovering right at the edge only to be tipped over as the tiny Helbing stabbed his knee. Balance lost, the Sargent fell back towards the courtyard below with a scream.

Shouts from below accompanied the thud, but neither Adventurer paused. Their job was to injure, cripple - kill if possible – the Archers. But most importantly, they had to distract them long enough for the teams.

Breath exploding from her nose, tail curled up against her body, the Catkin danced.

***

Daniel snarled as he deflected the sabre cut struck at his head. However, his defense left him open to the attack from the raptor, a clawing strike that raked alongside his breastplate. The screech of claw on metal made Daniel wince, but he crouched lower to regain his balance. Even as he did so, another arrow landed on the shield he still kept alleviated over Tula's crouched form.

"Lizard death," Tula snarled and released the draw on her bow. The arrow flashed forwards, the arrow punching through thick scales to pierce the raptor's chest. The raptor hopped backwards, taking its rider with him and roared in anger.

"Thanks," Daniel panted out, shifting the shield slightly to check for more attackers. Unfortunately, the four riders kept circling, forcing Daniel and Camilo to constantly shift their defense. Even with the continuing fire from the archers, the cavalry members continued to harass them. Even at the risk of taking arrows to the tail or shoulder.

"They've stopped," Casey said with a grin. Instead of firing on the raptors and their riders that surrounded them, Casey fired a flame-filled arrow at the second group of cavalry reinforcements. His burning arrow sunk into the chest of a rider, sending him sprawling to the ground and screaming as the Orc's flesh burned. Even then, the charging reinforcements looked unstoppable.

Daniel sucked in another breath, lowering the shield slightly to release the ache in his arm. Just in time to see another raptor rider duck in, a sabre swinging for his body. Just before it landed, a roar from the treetop distracted the Raptor Rider, offering Daniel time to raise his shield and lash out with **Perrin's Blow** to shatter the raptor's chest and throw its rider off.

"Omrak." Daniel breathed in relief. He did not need to turn around to know that the team which had hidden at the edge was now rushing out, crossing the distance to lend their aid. As the raptor struggled to its feet, Daniel lashed out with his foot and kicked it to the ground again. Letting his foot drop on the squirming monster, Daniel spun the spike on his hammer into the creature's skull. The dazed Raptor Rider slowly sat up, only to take an arrow to his face from a waiting Tula.

"Heal!" Camilo cried out, making Daniel turn as he retreated back to reinforce their line. Tula darted back too, nocking another arrow as Daniel turned to look.

"Damn it. Guard!" Daniel said. Once Camilo readied his spear to cover both sides, Daniel ducked low and placed his hand against Casey's exposed leg, forming the spell in his mind. **Moderate Healing** took longer to cast than **Minor Healing**, but it had the benefit of fixing larger and nastier wounds. Like the cut that ran from just above Casey's neck all the way down to his hip, tearing through the light armor that he had worn as though the leather armor had been cloth itself.

Power pulsed through the archer's body, making him shudder. First, blood stopped pumping for a brief moment as the wound began to close and heal at a visible rate. Guided by Daniel's knowledge, nerves, veins and arteries connected first before the muscle that connected it all began to grow. Wounds stitched themselves together as new cells linked, forming weak, newly healed muscles. With a shudder, Casey started breathing again as blood flowed through his body.

Daniel's lips thinned, professionally eyeing the wound and dissatisfied, he threw a **Healer's Mark** on the archer before he stood again to face their opponents.

By his side, Tula was panting, her arms trembling as exhaustion overtook her. Numerous arrows littered the area in front of them, a testament to the overuse of her Skills and the desperate defense she had put up in the short while that Daniel was distracted.

"Rest. I got this," Daniel said as he stepped forwards, eyeing the trio of riders left. If this kept up, he might need to use his last trick.

***

Omrak roared as he charged, feet pounding on soft earth as he neared the cavalry group. The Sargent snarled, gesturing quickly. Immediately, a pair of them shifted their direction, heading straight for the Northerner who had outpaced the remainder of the teams. Behind, he knew that the remainder of the Fallen Leaves were following, but the Northerner refused to slow down. If the cavalry reinforcements managed to make it to his friends, it would be over. Better for him to get injured than let that happen.

Seconds flashed past, and within moments, Omrak found the raptors nearly on him. A quick sideways hop took him out of range of the first but ensured that he had nowhere to go when the second Raptor Rider's sabre swung at him. A hasty block sent him stumbling backwards, a claw raising a bloody wound on his arm as the raptor rode past. Luckily, his new Skill had toughened his skin or else the injury would have been greater and potentially crippling.

"Close enough. **Fight me!**" Omrak roared, having eyeballed the distance. A pulse of power carried his words through all those around, drawing the attention of the remaining members of the cavalry who immediately turned their raptors. Even the couple of Orcs who resisted the provocation could do little as the mindlessly aggressive raptors swung their bodies towards the Northerner.

Raptors surrounding him, Omrak felt his heartbeat speed up, adrenaline flooding his system. Even the pain from the initial wound faded, and the blond Adventurer found himself smiling.

"Come. Let us seek the hallowed halls." Omrak exhaled as he swung his greatsword in an overhand block before drawing the sword into a quick riposte.

***

"Are they all insane?" Gerardo snarled. He quickly raised his sword up to the side and then slashed downwards, a crescent of blue light flowing from the strike to fly towards a surprised raptor. Cut across its back, the raptor reared backwards, forcing its rider to struggle to keep his balance.

The leader of the Fallen Leaves picked up speed once his Skill had finished, rushing towards Omrak. Even as he did so, he saw a wash of power bathe the Northerner, his fast-accumulating wounds healing slightly as Daniel's **Healer's Mark** triggered. A moment later, Eiju waved his hand, finishing his own spell of blessing and bathing the Northerner with a buff to his defense.

"Just Omrak," Rob answered.

Gerardo did not deign to reply, nor did Farhad. In a second, the warrior clad in his flowing robes had sped up, **Flash Stepping** his way towards the nearest raptor rider. Rather than throwing a straight cut, Farhad jumped into the air and spun. His sword held straight out from his body, he sliced across the Raptor Rider's body as he spun, the second blade cutting across the raptor's body as he landed. A leg dropped and Farhad continued to spin, dancing along the edges of the encirclement.

As Farhad's initial victim fell, Gerardo and the rest of the team reached the group. Gerardo **Shield Bashed** the raptor, throwing the already unstable Raptor Rider to the ground before he stabbed his blade into the raptor to finish it off. Eiju, beside them, ducked to the side of the dueling pair to finish the unraptored rider as he struggled to his feet.

Behind, Rob and Kelly had stopped a safe distance from the riders, their hands weaving lesser spells to distract and injure the riders. And in the centre of the battle, Omrak stood, glowing red and bleeding, his greatsword weaving in circles to strike and injure the raptors as they neared him.

***

That one. Omrak grinned as he blocked the cut, sliding the sabre over his right shoulder before he twisted his wrists and counter-cut against the Rider. The Rider ducked out of the way easily, but his motion blocked another Orc from approaching, allowing Omrak to hop lightly to the side.

"Come!" Omrak roared, pulling his sword back towards left shoulder with his false edge leading. He wanted, no, needed to finish off the Rider Sargent. Both he and his raptor were buffing the entire cavalry group, making them stronger, faster and more co-ordinated. Slaying the Sargent would provide the greatest benefit. And Omrak would be able to test himself against the Sargent.

Taking up Omrak's challenge, the raptor charged directly at the Northerner before its legs bunched and leapt. Cursing, Omrak threw himself back while cutting down only to have his sword blocked by the Sargent. As he landed, his backward momentum was halted by a strike to his back.

"Aaargh!" Omrak screamed, even as he felt the belt slung over his shoulder slide off his body, the strap cut.

The Sargent gave Omrak no time to rest as the raptor charged forwards. A quick sidestep allowed Omrak to avoid being bowled over, but he could do nothing to stop the claws that tore at his chest, battering his armor and leaving instant bruises beneath. Nor could the Northerner dodge the punch that slammed into his cheek, cracking the skin over his cheekbone. Still, it was a good trade compared to the sword on the other side.

Omrak had sacrificed his defense for an opportunity, and injured or not, he would not let it pass. His left hand flashed out and took hold of the back of the Sargent's belt. With a mighty heave, the giant Northerner yanked him from the raptor. Even as he did so, he screamed as he felt his back and shoulder muscles tear. The Sargent slammed into the ground, his abrupt shift in elevation and direction punching the air from his lungs.

For a second, Omrak staggered as he reoriented himself. Pain washed over him and then faded as a pulse from the **Healer's Mark** ran through his body. Omrak brought his sword up to guard, readying himself for another attack when he realised that the other Riders were busy, no longer focused on him. With a grin, Omrak set upon the Sargent, his greatsword darting forwards.

"Time to finish this!" Omrak snarled.

***

"Aieeee!" Asin screamed as she dropped, the forty feet between her and the ground rushing towards her with each passing second.

"Wooohooo!" Rita screamed beside her, the Helbing falling with Asin. A moment before the pair landed, a flare of power rushed through their bodies, pushing against gravity. The potion of air cushioning activated as the extended aura around their body touched the ground, triggering the spell.

Even so, the pair landed heavily. Asin crouched as she landed, her legs splayed apart slightly as the fall impacted her joins and the springy muscles of her Beastkin form. Unlike humans, the Catkin was actually lighter than you would expect for her size with a greater number of long muscle fibres, giving her some of the same feline ability to jump and land from great heights. Rita, on the other hand, slammed into the ground and rolled, tucking into a bowl and absorbing the impact in that way.

As the pair stood up, the remaining Archers from above began to fire arrows down at the pair of Adventurers. Not that the attacks were accurate. Angle and injuries hampered the Archers as did the loss of their Sargent. Still, Asin sniffed, it was not wise to wait around. Bounding forwards, the pair headed towards where their friends still fought, though the battles themselves looked to be winding down. Out of the corner of her eye, Asin noted the presence of a series of infantry troops rushing out to join the battle. Too little, too late.

***

The shock from a cut ran all along Daniel's arm, the empowered attack almost breaking through his defense. Shoving back against the attack, Daniel took a step forward and swung his hammer low, cracking the top of the Orc's thigh. Daniel grunted, hating the fact that he missed the knee, but he shifted his attention as the Orc Rider retreated.

Tula was doing fine, working her knife along the necks and tendons of the fallen raptors. Covering her and Camilo was Casey, his bow no longer spitting elementally empowered arrows. Still, the constant harassment and their initial losses left only a single other Raptor Rider and a single raptor alive. As Camilo spun his spear, feinting a cut before reversing the strike to lash the raptor across its throat, that number dropped again.

More importantly, none of the three sported more than minor wounds. Omrak, on the other hand, sported numerous cuts across his body as he limped forwards in his battle against the Rider Sargent. Shoving his shield forwards to force his own opponent backwards, Daniel hopped back and crouched behind his shield as he channeled his

Minor Healing II spell towards his friend. That none of the other fighters in the Fallen Leaves were badly injured was a testament to their style, patience and the overwhelming numbers they had brought against the cavalry.

"Careful!" Casey said as he sent an arrow blowing right past Daniel's nose. The healer jerked backwards, barely containing his spell as the arrow embedded itself in the cheek of the Orc that had charged forwards. Head snapped back from the force of the arrow, the Orc landed on the ground where Daniel crushed it with the edge of his shield as he finished the spell.

"Thanks!" Daniel said. He lifted and brought the shield edge down again, this time on the Orc's neck to finish it off.

"Time to go," Casey said, turning towards the incoming infantry platoon. An empowered fire arrow left his bow, only to land on a raised shield. It seemed that the spearmen in this fort carried the useful defensive equipment and knew how to use them.

"But…" Daniel looked worriedly at Omrak's group, only to see the Rider Sargent stumble as a pair of darts burrowed into his back. His distraction was sufficient to allow Omrak to swing his greatsword, lopping off his head with a mighty strike.

"Can he run?" Casey said. There was no need to say who.

"Probably," Daniel said, assessing the Northerner with his eyes and the weight of experience. Omrak was strong and stubborn enough to last.

"Then so should we," Casey snapped. Together, the group hurriedly grabbed the few Mana stones that had appeared and took off running for the woods. Meeting the infantry squad right now was not part of the plan.

Chapter 14

An hour and a half later, the teams had regrouped farther down the hill. It was with the return of Asin and Rita - who had been watching the infantry patrol, recover and return to the fort - that Gerardo finally felt that it was time to call for another meeting.

"That went well," Gerardo said simply.

"Dangerous," Daniel said with a grimace. He had just finished bandaging everyone up, having used up the greater portion of his Mana on **Healer Mark** spells. For now, keeping a small reserve was a necessity just-in-case the Orcs decided to pursue them. Though, he hoped, the ambushes conducted previously kept them wary.

"We lost no one. And other than your barbarian, none of us received severe injuries," Gerardo said.

"I am no barbarian. That is a Class that I have not achieved," Omrak said.

Gerardo waved Omrak's objection away before he continued. "According to Rita, there is both an Archer Sargent and an Infantry Sargent. Mini-bosses that need dealing with."

"Archer survived?" Asin said with a sniff.

"He did. Or he was moving at least," Rita confirmed. "Didn't see him on the walls though. But they've switched out the majority of the watch to infantry anyway."

"Smart," Tula commented. When Omrak shot her a look of puzzlement, she smiled and explained. "We crippled and injured their Archers. If they left the Archers out there, Casey and I could finish them off given enough time." Tula shot an envious glance over to Casey's bow before she continued, "This way, they can watch for us and only risk their more numerous infantry."

"And snipe at us with their hidden archers," Casey added. "We'll have to check to see if they're hiding outside the forest before we try anything further."

Gerardo nodded before he tapped his fingers. "We managed to cripple their archers and their cavalry. I say we continue to attack them."

"And if they refuse to come out again?" Daniel said. Without their cavalry, it was unlikely the Orcs would be willing to attempt to rundown Tula and Casey again. The fact that they had been willing to even try the first time was due to overconfidence, one that had occurred because each fort seemed to be operating entirely independently of each other. If not, using the same tactics over and over again would likely have failed.

Well, that and Casey's bow. Being attacked by an enchanted bow probably put a damper on their enthusiasm at being shot at.

"We'll pin them down and climb up," Gerardo said. "There are enough of us that if we can take part of the wall, we should be able to hold it."

Daniel nodded slowly. That was true enough. The biggest concern with holding the wall were archers who could range on them without fear and the constant pressure of the infantry. On the narrow walkways, together, the odds would drop from ten to one to five to one. With superior skill and Levels, they should be able to hold.

"Any objections?" When none cropped up, Gerardo nodded. "Then we begin tomorrow."

***

A day later, the group found themselves seated at the edge of the clearing, watching the fort. Rather than Orcs standing watch over the walls, they stared at a desolate, empty fort. Even Tula and Casey, with their respective farsight Skills, could not pick out any monsters.

"What do you think?" Gerardo said, frowning.

"They've pulled back," Rob said.

"But why?" Gerardo said.

"A losing proposition," Daniel said softly, eying the building. It made sense, at least to him. With two archers and the pair of shield-bearers, the group could pick off any Archers or Infantry that stood on the walls. Knowing that, and without their cavalry, the Orcs were better off staying off the walls. They might even decide to stay in the fort itself, giving their Archers a field of fire into the courtyard and the walls while forcing the Adventurers to contend with walls that refused to fall.

"We go in?" Omrak said as he pulled his sword out of the sheath before resheathing it.

"We go in," Daniel agreed. Gerardo opened his mouth to protest but then shut it, shaking his head only slightly. In the end though, whatever their personal feelings about the risk involved, they had no choice.

Of course, they did not just plan to go directly in. Safeguards were needed to allow the group to retreat in the case of overwhelming force or an unexpected level of resistance. Plans had to be made on who went in first, how they would go in and what objectives they were to complete. And, most importantly, they had to decide how they were going to breach that final defense – the gates of the fortress itself.

For that, Rob, Kelly, Eiju and Casey were tasked with using their magical expertise and Casey's bow to develop a solution.

Plans made, the group got to work.

***

To start with, the entire group decided to move up towards the wall. While the rest of the team waited below, Asin and Rita climbed the wall again. Tula and Casey kept an eye a short distance away on both the wall and the front gate, in case the Orcs decided to sally forth. A few tense minutes later, the pair had quietly ascended the wall to find the rampant and courtyard empty. Having planned for that eventuality, the pair moved immediately to the front gates after signalling their findings to the group below.

As the pair headed for the front gates, so did the group below. They moved quickly and smoothly co-ordinating their pace as best as they could. Even if there was a trap for their scouts at the gatehouse, the Adventurers would face it together.

At least, that was the thinking they had beforehand. Unfortunately, none of that mattered when the pair came to the gatehouse and found neither Orcs nor traps. Puzzled, the duo double-checked everything once more before they finally made their move, working the crank to raise the heavy bar that blocked their way. Whether by design or plain inattention to detail, the crank and its chains creaked and groaned as they worked, alerting the Orcs within the fort. In seconds, arrows began to fall around the pair working the crank.

"I'll cover, you keep cranking!" Rita said after a moment. The fact that the Helbing was of little use in working the crank was rather apparent, the small Adventurer having to leap into the air and use her body weight to help turn the crank at the required intervals.

Decision made, the Helbing pulled forth a large kit shield, a defense that literally dwarfed her body and which she used to help shield the Catkin. Even then, her small stature and the number of arrows falling meant that Asin would be sure to be hit at some point. Already, Asin was bleeding from a pair of shallow wounds.

"HELP!" Rita called out. "Help!"

A few seconds later, her cries for aid were answered as a ghostly, magical hand appeared. The hand quickly gripped the bar and helped raise it, the additional leverage making Asin's job easier. However, the Catkin could not help but snarl slightly as an arrow buried itself in her shoulder, almost making her lose her grip on the crank.

"Damn. Sorry!" Rita said. After eyeballing the damage, the Helbing grimaced and said. "Hold on. This is going to hurt."

"Wha- AAARGH!" Asin cried out in pain as Rita yanked the arrow out before pouring a healing potion on her arm.

"Back to work," Rita said.

Snarling, the Catkin's tail lashed out behind her before a near miss made the Catkin curl the tail up behind her body once more. Focusing on the crank, she worked it faster till the bar was fully elevated.

"Done!"

"About time," Rita said. Shoving the shield upright, Rita spun around, grabbed the iron bar that held the crank in place and slammed it into place. As an arrow cracked into the ground next to the newly exposed Helbing, she added. "Time to run!"

"Yes!" Asin said, already loping away without prompting.

***

Outside, Daniel jittered as he listened to the continuous thuds of arrows landing, the yelps and occasional cries of pain from his friends. Beside him, Rob had his eyes closed as he focused on the **Magic Hand** spell, only to snap it open after a second.

"Done!" Rob cried.

"Push!" Gerardo commanded. Together, the group put their backs into the gate, pushing to swing the gates open. It was only Kelly who stood aside, her eyes glowing with power as she held the edges of her spell together, waiting.

"My turn," Kelly said when the gap between the gates opened far enough. Seeing the distance offered, she released her spell. Fire raged in front of the fortress, heat and flames dancing in the air briefly. Unlike the first time she had cast the spell, Daniel noted that this one was filled with a greater degree of flame and noise but it died quicker too.

As the Archers recovered from the sudden assault, the group finally opened the gap in the gates wide enough. Daniel and Gerardo ducked within, hefting their shields into place as they moved to guard their friends from the archers. Meanwhile, the remaining members of the team

---

continued to push the gate apart, ensuring they had a wide-open line of retreat.

"Where is she?" Daniel said, eyes darting from side-to-side as he searched for the Catkin. A low yowl caught his attention and Daniel found himself spotting the Catkin who had found herself a barrel of water to hide behind. Held close to her was the injured Helbing, a pair of arrows stuck in her body.

"Rita!" Anguish filled Gerardo's voice when he saw the state of the Helbing. He glanced over to Daniel, his eyes growing wide and a silent please in them.

"On it!" Daniel said, already channelling a **Minor Healing II.** Even if it was a highly inferior spell, the advantage of being able to cast the spell from a distance was too great to ignore, especially in a time like this. As the spell rushed forth from his hand, he felt a pair of hard impacts on his shield and another on his greaves. Once again, Daniel thanked Erlis that he had managed to find that Quest. Being a melee healer without armour would have been suicidal otherwise.

"Go!" Camilo commanded Daniel even as Tula and Casey, freed from their job of pushing the gate, returned fire at the archers. Immediately, the Orc Archer's rate of fire and accuracy dropped as they began to worry over their own lives. With Camilo taking his place, Daniel took off running, skidding to a stop next to the injured pair.

"About time," Asin said. A gauze bandage was pushed against the wounds around Rita's body, but the bandage itself was soaked through. "Pull?"

"On my mark. Both of them," Daniel said, hand moving to rest against Rita's body. "Now!" With arrows pulled, Daniel cast his **Moderate Healing** spell, repeatedly layering the spell. Wounds began to close, but he grimaced as he realised that both arrows had managed to severe major arteries. Thankfully, both ends had curled up, reducing the blood loss. But still, his spells were not going to be enough. Not unless…

Daniel looked up, his eyes wide as he met Asin's. She offered him the barest of nods, and he reached deeper even as she slipped away to stand guard. His Gift unfolded from within his body, wrapping itself around the Helbing.

Every cut artery, a memory. Every torn vein, an experience. Torn muscles, an evening with Kh'yra. A severed tendon, an hour in the mines. Each passing wound, a portion of his life, of his memory. It filled his mind with gaps, with holes. Sometimes, sometimes, it felt like all that he had been, all that he was could pass through his fingers into another. His 'Gift'.

A shuddering breath, a cough. Daniel pulled back, letting his Gift wrap around him again as he turned back to his spells. This time around, the **Moderate Healing** spell worked even better than before. For this time, he knew her body, knew her physiology intimately.

"That hurt!" Rita complained as she touched the still raw wounds.

"Hold still and stay hidden. I'm going to add a **Healer's Mark** to patch you up, but any major movements and you're going to reinjure yourself," Daniel commanded.

"Can do! But, are you okay? You're looking a little pale," Rita said, squinting at Daniel through the slits in his helmet.

"I'm fine." Daniel brushed away her concern as he stood. He was fine. It was not as if he had not sacrificed his memories for others before. He just wished he knew what it was that he had lost...

His musings were torn away by the punishing impact of an arrow that landed directly on his armor. He staggered backwards, looking down long enough to see that the arrow had not punched its way through. Raising his shield, Daniel chose to run forwards with it, eyeing the scene of the battle.

Not much of one really, as Tula exchanged fire with the pair of remaining Archers. Now that Daniel had started paying attention again, the Archers turned their attention back to the mages who hid behind Omrak.

"How did you find a door?" Daniel exclaimed as he ran up to help his friend.

"Stable," Omrak grunted, holding the piece of wood up in front of the mages. As Omrak finished speaking an arrow crashed through the wood, leaving its head sticking out inches from Omrak's face. "Faster please, Hero Mages!"

The mages ignored Omrak, squatted silently behind and focused on their spells as they were. Daniel glanced down at the small enchanted ball that had been grafted onto the arrow where the pair of Mages were pouring their Mana into, weaving spell and enchantment. While inconvenient to form now, it would have been even more inconvenient to carry around the highly volatile and explosive sphere. Beside the mages, pouring in his Mana as well was Eiju, though, by his own admission, his Spells leaned towards buffs. Still, it didn't seem to matter.

"Tula? Anytime now…" Daniel called out while the rest of the team took shelter in what little cover there was — mostly behind the various individuals with shields.

"Trying!" Tula said after she loosed another arrow. This time around, a scream soon followed after. The Ranger grinned before letting out a little yelp when an arrow skipped off the ground to embed its tip in her calf.

"Damn it," Gerardo cursed as he watched the arrow bypass his defense. No matter how skilled, being shot at enough, some point the defense would fail. Which was why the mages and their plan was so important.

"Ready!" Rob called out as the Mana suppliers removed their hands from the vicinity of the arrowhead. Casey nodded and lifted his bow, humming slightly as he activated it.

"Moving… now!" Omrak roared, twisting his body aside and taking the door out of the way. His view clear, Casey loosed the multi-enchanted arrow-sphere. It flew through the air, cutting across space so fast it left a glowing line of power behind it until it impacted the door. And stuck.

"Uhh…" Daniel said, staring in incredulity at the glowing arrow. Then he noticed. The way the glow began to spread across the door, how it slowly intensified even as the tendrils of gold and red covered the surface of the entrance.

"Cover us!" Rob shouted. Omrak reacted immediately, pulling the door back over to the group. Daniel moved too, propping the door up with his shield in one corner before turning his head away. On instinct, he opened his mouth, moments before the explosion came.

Fire and fury, an impact that felt like being run over by a wagon. The door shattered, wooden splinters flying through the air to shred muscle and skin, to tear and injure. Omrak screamed, his body taking the brunt of the damage. Daniel too, but his better armor, his better position saved him. And behind them, the vulnerable mages sheltered.

"Move, move, move!" Gerardo roared as the explosion ended. Daniel looked up, spotting the Orcs who had taken the brunt of the explosion behind the doors slowly getting to their feet. Then he turned, his eyes widening as he saw the pin cushioned, bloody Northerner next to him. His hand lashed out, his Gift reaching for the Northerner even as he wove his **Moderate Healing** spell.

"I live, Friend Daniel," Omrak said, blood dripping down one eye. He swiped the blood away, and Daniel noted that the Northerner did not move from his hand. He even drew a health potion from his belt, downing the precious potion as his wounds healed. "And my Skill saved me from the worst of it."

"Idiot," Asin growled as she bounced forwards. Close enough for her to throw, the Catkin jumped again, leaping into the air before she cast her **Fan of Knives** at the slowly recovering group of Orcs. Her throwing knives were beaten to the Orcs by a storm of arrows which injured and killed some. Asin's knives added to the death toll as did Casey's glowing arrows. But there so many.

Farhad and Gerardo entered at a run, and Eiju, having recovered, followed soon after. His friend healed as best as he could for now, Daniel threw one more **Healer's Mark** on Omrak before he rushed forwards beside the Northerner. Of course, the big Northerner quickly outpaced Daniel, but there were more than enough Orc Spearmen for them all.

"Break them up. Don't let them form!" Gerardo shouted orders to the group as he followed after Farhad, dispatching and keeping his teammate safe. His sword lashed out, his shield blocked and always, always, the pair kept moving forwards.

As fast as they were, Asin was ahead of them. She danced through the group, blades held in hand as she cut, stabbed and struck again and again. Each motion hit, sometimes drawing blood, sometimes bouncing off armor. But each blow brought with it a charge of electricity, shocking the Orcs and disrupting their recovery.

And between, more arrows fell.

Having reached the entrance hall of the fortress, Daniel took his time, finishing off Orc after Orc. Their longer spears were of less use, especially in the tighter quarters of the hallway and with their line disrupted. Again and again, his hammer rose and fell, smashing aside weak defenses and crushing bone and skin.

Omrak, on the other hand, rushed forwards, forming the third prong of the attack with Farhad and Eiju. Together, the trio cut into the Orcs while Gerardo did his best to keep them safe. Asin, by this time, had fallen back, her initial momentum no longer sufficient to deal with the recovering group. Behind, Tula and Casey were rushing forwards to get better angles to support the group while the mages recovered their Mana outside.

Parry. Strike. Parry. Strike. Strike. Dodge.

The rhythm of the battle took hold of Daniel as he pushed forwards, interrupted only occasionally as he checked on his friends. By now, the Orcs had reformed, leaving nearly half their number on the ground. But facing the hedgehog of spears and shields, the Adventurers found themselves at an impasse. One broken, not in their favor, as a roar from behind the group alerted the Adventurers of even more trouble.

"That's a big fella," Rita said, startling Daniel who had just finished his last opponent. He stood there, panting as he attempted to suck in more air into his lungs while staring at the latest addition to the battle.

Orc Lord (Floor Champion Level 19)
Health: 430/430

Taller than even Omrak, the Orc Lord must have been at least nine feet tall. A creature of muscle and fury, it strode forwards clad in a nearly full suit of plate mail wielding a great sword. It roared again and the black-skinned Orcs parted, allowing the Orc Lord to face them.

"Farhad, Omrak. The Lord," Gerardo snapped. "Eiju, Asin and I will guard you best we can. Daniel, keep us healed!"

Daniel grimaced at the words, staring at his Mana bar. Barely enough Mana to cast a single **Moderate** Healing spell left, after all the damage and spells he had cast. He debated using a **Healer's Mark** but discarded it. This battle would be over before the slow-healing regenerative spell would be ready.

"Come, monster. I challenge you!" Omrak said, a hand moving to his face to wipe at the blood that slowly trickled down towards his eye, the entirety of his body glowing red as the rage suffused and strengthened him. The Orc Lord growled in answer but suddenly jumped forwards, his sword coming down.

Hand still in the air wiping the blood away, Omrak was unable to block the blow. Luckily, Farhad reacted in time, throwing himself forwards and blocking the attack with his crossed swords. Borne under by the greater weight, Farhad sagged to his knees as he shed the greatsword to the side. Hand gripping the sword, Omrak roared and swung his sword, joining Farhad in battle.

At the same time, beside the main fight, the spearmen surged forwards. Working each corner, Gerardo and Eiju could only hold off the spears, blocking and parrying the attacks. Luckily, Tula and Casey had found new angles and sent their arrows down the range, providing a much-needed distraction. As did Rob's magically controlled spikes and the occasional flaming arrow from Kelly.

As for Daniel, he found himself the odd man out. His weapon was too short to aid in the crowded fight against the Orc Lord. He could not afford to move away from either of the melee fighters though as his most powerful healing spell was touch ranged. And engaging in battle with the deadly Spearmen would likely mean he might miss the opportunity to save a life.

"Ba'al's tears," Daniel cursed as he found himself behind the pair, waiting. He would step in when needed, with shield and hammer. He stood there, in perfect position to watch as the Orc Lord pounded his Northern friend and the dual-wielding, robe-wearing Adventurer.

"I will hold him!" Omrak panted out loud to Farhad. Daniel saw the Orc Lord's eyes narrow at Omrak's words but before he could warn his friend, Omrak had thrown a heavy strike at the other. Rather than parrying the blow, the Orc Lord stepped aside, dodging it and counter-striking Omrak.

Omrak grinned wide, throwing his entire body forwards as he brought the hilt of his sword up, catching the strike on his crossguard. Badly, as Omrak's momentum and the Orc Lord's strength pushed the cut into Omrak's arm, leaving a deep, bleeding wound.

"Now!" Omrak roared, pushing against the Orc Lord and trapping his sword against his body and sword. Farhad ducked low, cutting at the Orc Lord's legs and leaving bleeding wounds. Yet, it was insufficient for the monster roared, throwing Omrak back with a surge of strength. A foot raised and kicked outwards, catching Farhad in the face and tossing him back.

Into the gap, Daniel darted forwards. His shield blocked the next strike aimed at Omrak's head, his eyes narrowed as he swung his hammer at a hand. His **Find Weakness** Skill was screaming at him, telling him of the few weaknesses the monster. Too few, but the fingers were one of them.

Too bad the Orc Lord managed to twist his sword aside, blocking the blow and scraping Daniel's back. Grunting, Daniel **Shield Bashed** the monster as he staggered forwards, panting out loud as he gave himself a moment of rest.

"I am not done!" Omrak roared, his last healing potion bottle preceding the Adventurer's body. Farhad slunk sideways, tackling a Spearman that had found a gap with Eiju. Together, Daniel and Omrak attacked the Orc Lord, the trio trading minor wounds.

"Can't. Beat. Him," Daniel panted out. He had triggered Skill after Skill in an attempt to give them some advantage. But thus far, he had failed. The Orc Lord was stronger, faster and more importantly, not already winded by a fight beforehand. By his side, Omrak was even more tired, his attacks visibly slowed.

"Take the chance," Omrak replied. When the Orc Lord threw another cut at Daniel, Omrak blocked it with his own sword and shoved the monster backwards. This pushed him deeper into the Orc infantry's lines and exposed his side to a punishing kidney punch. But even as Omrak sagged, a grin split his face as he breathed the Skill activation out. **"The Lightning's Call."**

Channelling all the pain, all the injuries, all the anger that had built within him, Omrak unleashed the attack in the midst of the group. Even though he was deep in the lines, the lightning still reached out and struck his friends. Eiju, in the midst of a block, found his arm trembling as electricity arced through his body. So pure was the pain that he did not even notice the spear that tore open his shoulder blade. But worst of all was Daniel. Clad in full iron plate mail, the Adventurer was a lodestone to the lightning, a beacon for the attacks.

The Adventurer screamed as the pain assaulted his body, drove him to his knees. Blood filled Daniel's mouth as he bit his own tongue, his body shuddering as the electricity grounded itself through him. But, as Omrak knew, Daniel had an advantage. A Gift. And reaching within, forcing himself to push past the pain, the Adventurer sealed his screaming nerves, offering himself a moment's respite and focus.

"I. Call. You," Daniel breathed out, slamming the hilt of his hammer into the ground. The impact caused the hammer to glow, its summoning function finally activated. Daniel had been carrying that Boss Imp around with him for months now, refusing to use it due to the low probability of the 'capture' effect of the hammer triggering. But now, he had no choice.

As the healer collapsed to the ground, his Gift working overtime to slowly fix him, a cloud of red smoke rose from around the hammer. From the cloud, a large, muscular red figure wielding a whip could be seen. The Boss Imp grinned, needle-sharp teeth widening as it looked at the monsters around him.

"Free at last!" the Boss Imp roared and swung its whip at the nearest Orc Spearman, wrapping the end around its neck and pulling the poor, barely recovered creature to him. Gripping the ends of the whip, the Boss Imp twisted its hips, lifting the monster into the air by its neck before slamming the black-skinned Orc into the ground.

"Not what I had planned," Daniel muttered as he came to and looked around. Pushing his Gift back into place as his body stopped spasming, Daniel realised that the Boss Imp was busy tangling with the spearman rather than focusing on the Orc Lord like he had planned.

In fact, as his eyes widened, Daniel realised that the Orc Lord was beating on the weakly defending body of Omrak, the Orc Lord having lost his sword somewhere during the intervening period. As Daniel struggled to his feet, Eiju threw his spear at the Lord's back, the glowing spear piercing the monster's back and leaving a sickly green colouration.

A brief second later, a pair of arrows, one glinting red and one burning blue, slammed into the monster's back in rapid succession. The blue arrow froze the armor before the red arrow shattered it, sending shards of metal into the creature's back. As the monster roared, Rita appeared from the shadows, the tiny Helbing jumping into the air and plunging her dagger deep into its body before using her body weight to rip the wound open.

Bleeding and wounded, the monster backed off Omrak's prone form, only to be met by Daniel as he charged forwards. Triggering **Shield Bash** just before he slammed into the monster, Daniel and the Orc Lord fell backwards through the hallway door. A blow by the Orc Lord took away Daniel's hammer, and the pair began to grapple in earnest.

Old lessons from Angie came back to Daniel and the stout Adventurer began to maneuver for position. Pull hand away from the Orc Lord, put two limbs and body weight on one hand. No matter how strong the Orc Lord was, how large, he could not fight the combined strength of Daniel's entire body against one limb. Keep weight down, do not let the monster buck him. He almost failed at the last, but for the timely intervention of Rita. The Helbing had scurried forward through the hallway and planted her dagger in the Orc's calf, forcing it to spasm and kick her aside to smash into the wall.

Finally, with the arm in a lock, Daniel began the laborious process of twisting it. The Orc Lord was humanoid, and while its body structure was slightly different than a human's, it still had the same tendencies – including a maximum degree that its arm could twist in a certain direction. Focused as he was, Daniel had no time to pay attention to the others and could just hope that the rest of the team was doing well. Not that he had any Mana left to aid them.

With a crack and snap, the Orc Lord's arm finally gave way. Grinning savagely as the monster screamed, Daniel gave the damaged limb another yank as he moved, heading for the large creature's body. The pair rolled and fought, the Orc Lord growing progressively weaker as it bled out and was crushed by Daniel. And behind, Daniel finally caught a glimpse of the hallway where the Adventurers were slowly gaining the upper hand after Omrak's sacrificial attack.

Hand locked around the Orc Lord's neck, Daniel watched as the team kept the Spearmen engaged. Occasionally, one would break away in an attempt to get to their leader, but an arrow or throwing knife would always find them. In one corner, the Boss Imp engaged two different spearmen, its whip discarded as it lashed out with its claws while being stabbed repeatedly.

In time, the Orc Lord slowly stopped struggling and Rita made her way over to the unconscious monster to push a dagger into its chest. The monster gave one last convulsive twitch before it stilled, and Daniel clambered out from under the monster with effort.

As if the death of the Orc Lord had been the signal, the last defense of the stragglers collapsed. By the time the pair limped their way to the doorway of the entrance hall, the battle within it had finished. Eiju was crouched over a shallow breathing Omrak, slowly pouring a vial of healing potion down the bigger Adventurer's mouth.

"Injuries?" Daniel called out. Almost as one, the entire team raised their hand. Daniel winced, letting experienced eyes wander over the group, sorting serious injuries. Clapping his hands together, Daniel limped in. "Alright, let's get to work."

Chapter 15

"Floor stone!" Asin crowed, tossing the Mana Stone from one hand to another with a grin. The fist-sized Mana stone had an amazing clarity, one that Daniel had not seen but in the Guild itself as an example. He could not help salivating slightly at the coin that would generate when they made it back.

"Same!" Rita called out making Asin jerk her head to the side.

"And here too," Camilo called out, his spear propped to the side.

"Ditto," Rob added as he showed everyone his finding.

"That makes no sense," Daniel said.

The treasury they had located had four chests, the largest being the one that Asin had opened. Soon, the group had laid their findings down before Gerardo and Daniel. Four large Mana stones, Asin's the largest by far and then three smaller, but still large stones from the other chests. In addition, surprisingly, Asin's chest had included a small amulet - a medal that Rob and Kelly immediately declared magical. Rather than risk the medal binding to one of them or potentially being cursed, the group set the medal aside. While Panqua was not likely to curse an object, general wisdom held that it was better to check all magical equipment before use. On occasion, Ba'al's corruption could infiltrate Panqua's design.

"It might perhaps make more sense than you think," Rob said, stroking his beard. "We have yet to find a second staircase or portal. I might even conjecture that there is no such location."

"You're thinking we're on the third floor?" Kelly said, eyes going wide.

"Yes."

"But we never found the Floor Champion previously," Gerardo said and then glanced at Daniel who shook his head in negation.

"We did, however, fight three Sargents. Mini-Champions if you will," Rob said holding up his fingers. "We also fought the Orc Lord which is undoubtedly this floor's Champion."

"So, Panqua created a single large floor?" Kelly said slowly and then sat back thinking. "But separated each via invisible portals, allowing more Adventurers to explore. Though, we ended up travelling through the same forts often."

"A test," Rob said.

"Of what? Patience?" Gerardo said with a snort.

"Not of us. Of the floor," Rob said waving his hand around. "Any good Enchanter knows, you must test your formulas. A Dungeon design for Panqua is perhaps the same as for an arrow design would be for us. Just another day's work."

"And Artos is known to change," Kelly added slowly. "And it's long periods of quiescence."

"Exactly," Rob said.

"What does that mean for us then?" Gerardo impatiently interrupted. While the pair of Mages might be content to argue about the ramifications of the Dungeon design, the rest of the team was busy exploring the fortress once more, doing a much deeper check for the missing stairs or portal.

"We will know when the others come back," Kelly said.

"But if I had to make a guess, I would say that we will not be able to confirm anything till we leave the fortress," Rob added.

"Then let's get to searching," Daniel said and stood up, picking up the large Mana stone and tossing it to Asin. The Catkin grabbed it and put it away while the others took the ones assigned to them and set each aside. As the entire battle had been completed together, the group had already decided to pool the Mana stones and other equipment collected and sell them as a group to the Adventurers before splitting the final take evenly between the two groups.

In truth, as Daniel led the rest around to help check the fortress, he could not help but be slightly grateful. He knew the Fallen Leaves had more members, and thus an even split was actually more advantageous for their team. Yet, Gerardo had offered the even split immediately without hesitation. Even the man's overall demeanour had cooled slightly since the battle.

As Asin hopped along the wall, tapping against the stone with the hilt of her knife, her tail waving lazily behind her, Daniel smiled. Perhaps it was just that coin in one's purse always made others relax.

***

That evening, the group found themselves camped at their usual spot. By common agreement, the teams had decided that staying in the now-empty fortress was too creepy. Even if the beds looked entirely too comfortable. Still, with the threat of the Orcs defeated, that evening's meal was more joyous and celebratory than ever. Even if everyone still kept their voices down as a precaution, the mood among the group was certainly more joyous.

It was later at night when Daniel was leaning against a convenient boulder and staring out at the mist-filled darkness that Gerardo found him.

"Adventurer Chai," Gerardo said.

"Gerardo," Daniel greeted. Gerardo sat down next to Daniel who looked over at the fellow Adventuring leader expectantly.

"I came to apologise. And to thank you," Gerardo finally said. "Your team deserves to be here. Perhaps even more than mine. You are good, if raw. And brave."

"Sometimes too brave," Daniel said softly, recalling a bleeding Omrak. He rubbed his nose, a memory of the extensive internal injuries the damn Northerner had developed coming to mind. Forced healing through the healing potions was dangerous and with his extensive use in a short period, Omrak had managed to develop a number of deep, persisting injuries. Injuries that Daniel had mostly fixed with his Gift. Yet, he could not find it within himself to complain – without Omrak's bravery and sacrifice, they would never have won.

"Adventurer?" Gerardo said and Daniel's attention snapped back to the man.

"Sorry."

"No need. It has been a long delve," Gerardo said. He paused for a second before he added, "Thank you for what you did with Rita. And our injuries."

Daniel could not help but shrug. In the aftermath of the fight, Daniel had not been able to do much about magically healing everyone, his basic healing skills had been of use. That, and he had quietly used his Gift on a few of the more distressing injuries. Injuries that, even with magical healing, might not have been fixed properly especially if they were not dealt with soon enough. After all, spells like **Moderate Healing** could magically sew over wounds, but their effectiveness was dictated to some extent by the base knowledge of the caster. The spell was also less directed, often healing the entire body at a time rather than focusing on problem areas. His Gift, on the other hand, allowed him to directly fix problems.

"It's a pity finding a healer is so difficult. Perhaps it's time for me to spend more time learning the skill," Gerardo added, offering a half smile. After a second, he glanced over to the group, his voice lowering. "I looked over Rita's wounds. And what she described."

"Oh?"

"The healing…" Gerardo paused, then shook his head. "It should not be possible. But it happened."

"I did have to spend most of my Mana…"

"Most," Gerardo said, his lip quirking slightly. "But not all. What you did isn't something an Advanced Adventurer could do." For a moment Gerardo fell silent before he slapped the ground, pushing upwards. "I don't really know what you did. I'm not sure I want to. But I'm glad you were here and that you're one of us. We'll keep your secret." At that, Gerardo flicked a glance to where the members of the Burning Fields sat, chatting quietly with one another. "But I'd be careful."

Daniel stared at Gerardo for a second, his eyes narrowing before the Adventurer finally nodded. It was only when Gerardo had left that he slumped slightly, concern growing in his eyes. It was something he had always feared, his Gift getting out. At some point, it would no longer be possible to hide it. Thankfully, Gerardo seemed willing to let things go. But sooner or later…

Sooner or later, Daniel would have to decide between his privacy and allowing someone to die. And Daniel knew the decision he would make. In the end, for him, there really had never been a decision. Not in a long time.

***

"That's it?" Gerardo said, his eyes wide. Daniel found himself next to the leader, the pair of them standing at the entrance to the small building that enclosed the Dungeon portal. The two frowned, turning around and bumping into the exiting other Adventurers. Chuckling ruefully, the pair moved away even as exclamations of surprise resounded through the room.

"We just left the hill…" Omrak muttered out loud.

"What hill, Adventurer?" the Guild Master asked, standing at the entrance with his hands clasped behind his back. The tense Adventurers, having just left a Dungeon predictably reacted with some cursing and knee-jerk reactions, drawing or aiming them before they realised who it was and stopped.

"Guild Master," Daniel greeted.

"Good. That's two groups," the Guild Master said, his eyes sweeping over the Adventurers. "And no losses. Clean yourself up; we have the inn across the street. Report what you have found afterwards."

The group looked around, frowning as they stared at the Guild Master. After a brief moment, Gerardo finally spoke up. "Guild Master, is there something wrong?"

"Many things. But the Yellow and Green groups have yet to return," the Guild Master replied, his face drawn tight.

His pronouncement made the group draw in a deep breath of shock. If any group were to be expected to fail, it would have been theirs. And worse, they knew how hard their own floors had been. What changes, what difficulty did the other groups face? And what did that failure mean for them and for Silverstone?

Author's Note

If you enjoyed reading the book, please do leave a review and rating. Not only is it a big ego boost, it also helps sales and convinces me to write more in the series!

If you enjoyed this, check out my other series:
-          Life in the North (An Apocalyptic LitRPG)
https://readerlinks.com/l/729295
-          A Gamer's Wish (An Urban Fantasy LitRPG)
https://readerlinks.com/l/729151
-          A Thousand Li (a cultivation series inspired by Chinese wuxia and xianxia novels)
https://readerlinks.com/l/729231

For more great information about LitRPG series, check out the Facebook groups:
  - Gamelit Society
https://www.facebook.com/groups/LitRPGsociety/
  - LitRPG Books
https://www.facebook.com/groups/LitRPG.books/

About the Author

Tao Wong is an avid fantasy and sci-fi reader who spends his time working and writing in the North of Canada. He's spent way too many years doing martial arts of many forms and having broken himself too often, now spends his time writing about fantasy worlds.

If you'd like to support him directly, Tao now has a Patreon page where previews of all his new books can be found!

- https://www.patreon.com/taowong

For updates on the series and the author's other books (and special one-shot stories), please visit his website: http://www.mylifemytao.com

Subscribers to Tao's mailing list will receive exclusive access to short stories in the Thousand Li and System Apocalypse universes: https://www.subscribepage.com/taowong

Or visit his Facebook Page: https://www.facebook.com/taowongauthor

About the Publisher

Starlit Publishing is wholly owned and operated by Tao Wong. It is a science fiction and fantasy publisher focused on the LitRPG & cultivation genres. Their focus is on promoting new, upcoming authors in the genre whose writing challenges the existing stereotypes while giving a rip-roaring good read.

For more information on Starlit Publishing, visit our website!
https://www.starlitpublishing.com/

You can also join Starlit Publishing's mailing list to learn of new, exciting authors and book releases.
https://starlitpublishing.com/newsletter-signup/

Read an excerpt of Book 6 of Adventures on Brad series:
The Forest's Silence

Chapter 1

Daniel sat at the table on the second floor of a tavern, staring at the gate that once sent him and his party members into a Dungeon. A few weeks later, there were wooden barricades blocking exit from the entrance, and stone walls were fast forming behind those temporary barricades. Adventurers stood at attention behind the wooden barricades while even more city guards waited.

Daniel ran a hand through his black hair, his brown eyes tightening in memory over the last few weeks. The wooden barricades were the first thing to arrive, but soon after, the Adventurers Guild had started rotating Indigo and Violet teams to watch over the Dungeon entrance. Aided by the city guards, the goal was to stem any attacks that might arise.

"Anything?" Asin asked, her bestial growl erupting from her throat in a low purr. The Catkin sat down next to Daniel, long ears twitching as she peered out the window. Claws extended and retreated on her furry palms. Daniel looked away to meet Asin's violet eyes and shook his head.

"Do not worry. They are a strong team," Omrak said, sitting down. Yet, even the giant Northerner's usual good cheer was subdued, his words carrying little weight of conviction in them. In truth, no one held any further hope for the teams to exit the Dungeon. Too much time had passed. Food would have run out, and potions of healing and mana would be depleted. If they were still alive, any sensible team would have withdrawn.

Knowing that, the Adventurers Guild had taken action. It was their job to deal with Dungeons. Failure to do so meant that an outbreak would occur – especially in Artos. The Dungeon only appeared once in a while, allowing a small number of teams in before it shut down again. But now, it had appeared earlier than normal and had not been cleared. The Guild could no longer rely on past practice. And so, they watched and waited.

A thump next to Daniel took his attention away from the table. Tula set her plate of food down beside Daniel—the roasted vegetable, fresh bread and meat-filled stew setting his stomach rumbling. Daniel looked up, flashing Tula a quick smile. The Ranger returned the smile, her placid brown eyes given a sinister air from the small scar that bisected one eyebrow. "Don't mind me. Just had to grab a bite to eat when I smelled what they were cooking."

"I do not understand how you can eat that," Rob said, sniffing slightly. The Selkie's dark, oily hair caught the light as he joined the group, calloused hands cupping a mug of ale. "Their drinks are barely acceptable."

"Tastes fine to me," Tula said around a mouthful of food. "Eaten a lot worse on the road."

"Ugh. Rangers." Rob sniffed but then turned his gaze over to the window. "Any change?"

Around them, the tavern buzzed with more business than it had seen in years. The tavern and the one across the street had become unofficial hangouts for many Adventurers with nothing better to do. A shared sense of loss and hope, of responsibility and burden, kept them close at hand in case the worse came to be. Yet...

"No." Daniel shook his head and gulped down a mouthful of beer. Rob was right—the beer here was barely acceptable. Nowhere as good as Erin's. But they did not come here for food.

"I was thinking we should try Portos next," Rob said, leaning forwards. "We're stalled on the fourth floor of Aramis right now, so we should do Portos. New monsters mean more experience. Might get us over the hump we need to level up."

"We've only run the fourth floor five times," Omrak rumbled. "It is insufficient to work out the proper methods to clear the floor. It only requires perseverance!"

"Sure, sure. I get that," Rob said. "But I'm just saying, we could run Portos and level up, make it down a couple of floors. Earn a little coin. Then tackle Aramis again in a better situation."

"I do not like giving up."

"Rob's not saying give up, just stop for a bit. And…" Tula paused and then ducked her head, sipping on the stew. Daniel cocked his head to the side, surprised that the Ranger had suddenly stopped talking. That was very strange.

"Ow!" Daniel exclaimed, glaring at Asin who had kicked him under the table. Still, he got the point. "What is it, Tula?"

"Nothing. Well, nothing right now…" Tula paused, visibly hesitant and then sighed. "But I got to go soon. In a week or so. There's a new expedition leaving Silverstone, and I've been requested to join it."

"What?" Daniel said.

"Luz's starry beard!" Omrak exclaimed.

"Oh…" Rob said.

"Yes. Sorry. Told you this was a short-term assignment. I've liked working with you all, really. But cities? It's not my thing, you know?" Tula said. "Rangers are meant to be in the forest. And this expedition is headed back towards my old village. Be nice to see my family again."

"That makes sense. Family is important," Daniel said, even as a flash of regret ran through him. He had none left now, making him just another adventuring orphan. There were a surprisingly large number of them. Or perhaps not so surprising when one considered the kind of job they took. It was easier to risk your life when you had nothing binding you close.

"Well, if you're leaving, that's all the more reason to do Portos!" Rob said, thumping his open hand on the table. "Otherwise Tula won't get the chance to see it. Or get the new monster experience."

That argument seemed to convince Omrak who rumbled his agreement. Asin just chuffed while Daniel scratched the side of his head, working out the timings. "When?"

"Tomorrow?"

"Can't do it. I promised time at the hospital," Daniel said, going over his own schedule. Since their successful run, Daniel had been flooded with offers to make use of his healing spells. Rather than constantly decline, Daniel had taken to working at one of Silverstone's hospitals part-time. There, he received a regular salary for his work, and the adventurers and Guilds were forced to pay the hospital direct. Since his schedule was publicly posted, the arguments over the use of his limited spells and Mana had dropped. It did not stop the invitations, but it had at least stemmed the flow somewhat.

"Fine. Day after," Rob said.

Murmured agreements broke out from around the table. Once that was done, Daniel started assigning roles to the party, ensuring that they worked together to not only stock and ready themselves for the new Dungeon but also gathered whatever information they could. After an agreement to meet again the next night to go over and plan the run, the group dissolved into cheerful bickering and reminiscing once more.

Yet, once in a while, one or the other of the party would look out the window, staring at the quiet Dungeon gate. Waiting.

Continue reading here:
https://readerlinks.com/l/960925

9 781989 458808